The Kalarthri

The Way to Freedom

Book One

H.M. Clarke

Also by H.M. Clarke

The Way to Freedom Series
1: The Kalarthri
1.1: The Cavern of Sethi
2: The Dream Thief
3. The Awakening
4. The Enemy Within
5. The Unknown Queen
6. The Searchers
7. The Whisperer
8. The Deceiver
9. The Great Game
10. The Gathering
The Complete Season One–Books 1 5
The Complete Season Two–Books 6-10

Coming Soon
11. The Mark of Fate

The Blackwatch Chronicles
1: Proven

Coming Soon
2: Uprising

The Verge
1: The Enclave

Coming Soon
2: Citizen Erased

H.M. CLARKE

The Order
1: Winter's Magic
Marion: An 'Order' Short Story

John McCall Mysteries
1: Howling Vengeance

The Kalarthri

The Way to Freedom

Book One

H.M. Clarke

Copyright © Text and Cover Illustration H. M. Clarke 2013

All rights reserved; No part of this publication may be reproduced or transmitted by any means, electronic, mechanical, photocopying or otherwise, without the prior permission of the copyright owner.

First published in The United States of America in 2013

Sentinel Publishing LLC, Dayton, Ohio

The moral rights of the author have been asserted.

DEDICATION

This book is dedicated to my two wonderful children. My son Keith and my daughter Ariadne.

CONTENTS

Acknowledgments

1 Leave-Taking

2 The Choosing

3 The Krytal

4 Kalena Kalar

5 Harada Thurad

6 Backlash

7 Night Wanders

8 Confessions

9 The Grand Tour

10 The First Flight

11 The Searchers

12 The Post House

13 The Lieutenant's Dilemma

14 Honor Debt

15 As Quiet as Mice…

ACKNOWLEDGMENTS

I thank all of my family and friends for getting me to this point and for their belief that I could finish this.

I especially thank my mum, Frances, and my son, Keith, for being such an inspiration

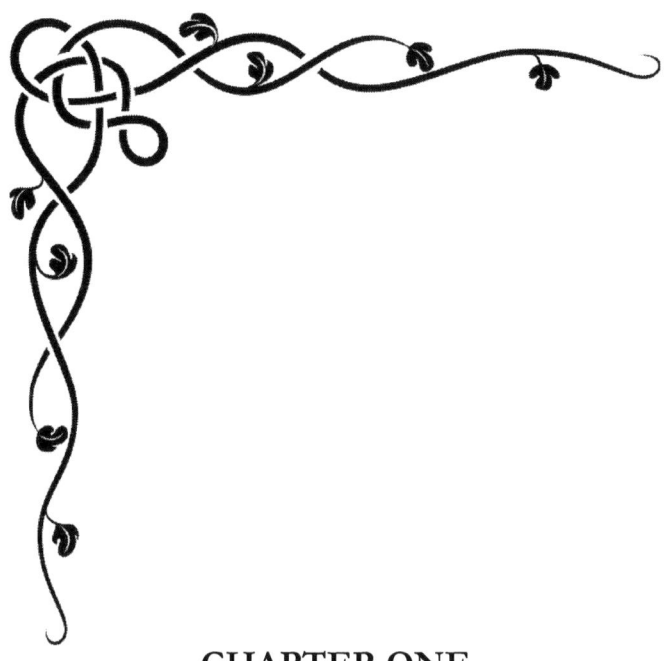

CHAPTER ONE

LEAVE-TAKING

Today was a special day.

Fields of wheat rippled in the morning breeze, their whiskery golden heads waving happily at the sun. In another week the harvest would begin and the fields would no longer be tall enough to hide in. Nearby, black-faced sheep bleated quietly to themselves as they cropped the spring grass. None of the adults would be working the fields or tending the flocks today and the children had been released from their duties. A shaggy sheepdog sat to one side keeping a watchful eye on his flock.

The day was warm, and the sky spread out above the village of Kurst like a blanket of blue wool. Large Eldar and Oak trees surrounded the fields and the village, some of which, if you climbed to the top, was large enough to see over the surrounding woods to the coast.

The young girl that now ran joyfully through Kurst main gates out into the early morning sun had this very thing in mind. Kalena wanted to be out before anyone else, she wanted to keep this day all to herself.

Last night while she lay in her cot, Kalena could hear her mother weeping and her father trying to comfort her. Both mama and papa had been upset since the messenger came to the town a few days ago. The taunts from Videan still rankled with her. He had been telling her for the past week that mama and papa were going to give her away. Kalena knew that her brother was only jealous because mama and papa paid more attention to her. But his teasing hurt. Kalena looked up to her older brother and would give nearly anything to have his respect. He seemed to think her a silly young girl. Just because she was ten, and he was fifteen did not mean she was silly!

Kalena laughed as she left the confines of the town, using the sound to push away her troubled thoughts and turned her feet towards the mass of grassland, wheat fields and trees that terminated at the steep cliff that fell into the Bay. Running through the flowers with her long hair streaming loose behind her like black silk; the front of her skirts caught up in her hands to prevent them tangling with her legs, she dashed past the trees, impulsively deciding to look at the sea instead from the cliff top. Clutched tightly in the crook of her arm was a small rag doll that her mother had made. It was well worn and well-loved and she never let it out of her sight. She kept running until the ground dropped away suddenly before her out of the wild mass of grasses and wildflowers.

Kalena threw herself down by the drop and untidily swung her legs over the edge to sit starring over the wide expanse of swirling ocean with Kala her doll propped up next to her.

The sea breeze danced merrily across the waves to play with the glittering expanse of sand that swept in a golden carpet to the stony cliff face. Sea birds floated gently with the wind or bobbed across the surface of the water, their calls drifting over the white-capped sea. To the north and west, the water stretched as far as the eye can see, but to the south loomed the large island of Monarstros that seemed to stand firm against the might of the sea. It was to this island that Kalena now gazed.

Kalena Tsarland sat staring wistfully at the island, wondering what it would be like to live there. Would it be different from her life at Kurst Village? What would the people be like? What would being on a boat be like? These questions circled around in Kalena's head every time she looked out to the island but as yet she had found no answers. Having never been away from the village or its surrounds Kalena looked excitedly to the time when she could travel and see the world. Even her parents have never been more than half a day's walk away from Kurst village. And that was only to trade with the fisher folk down the coast. Kalena indulged herself in a smile as she gazed across the sea.

"Kala, one day we'll go to that island and we'll meet lots of people and make lots of friends. And we'll meet boys who will not hide you in a feeding trough and not think we're silly."

Kalena fingered the mending on Kala's arm where a hungry sheep had started to munch before she rescued the doll from the trough. Her mother had stitched the hole and even put a bandage over it to help it get better. Kalena didn't speak to Videan for months after the incident. Not that he noticed.

Most of all Kalena wanted to have friends. There were not many children in the village that were her age, except for three boys. The girls either thought themselves too old to be seen with her or they were too young and not interested in what she liked to do.

One thing that she did notice was that the adults treated her and some of the other children differently. She couldn't quite put her finger on what was different, but they always seemed to receive extra attention from the adults. Well, the older children thought so. They were supposed to be able to get away with things more often as well. Kalena didn't think so. She had felt her father's hand on her bottom several times for her misdemeanors.

Sighing, Kalena pushed herself up from the cliff face. Grabbing Kala in one hand, she gave her skirts a quick brush with the other.

"Why don't we go to our tree?" Kalena asked her doll. She made Kala's head nod in agreement before scampering back across the wildflowers into the surrounding woods.

Kalena made her way across the bush lands quickly dodging between the trunks of Elder and Gum. She was heading towards a large, gnarled Coastgum tree that stood in the far corner of the Common Wheat field to the south of the village. As soon as she sighted the field between the trees, Kalena instinctively ducked down in the underbrush. She sat there listening a moment before she remembered that the adults would not be working today. Some of the village men did not approve of girls climbing in trees.

Feeling silly, she quickly sprinted the last distance before hiding behind the trunk of her tree, out of sight of the field.

Slowly Kalena peered around the wide bole of the tree to make sure that the fields were well and truly empty. Seeing that the coast was clear, she then tucked her doll into the band of her skirt and looked into the branches above her.

The Coastgum tree towered high above her. It was quite easily the tallest tree she had ever seen, and that was the main reason she chose to climb it. When she sat in its branches Kalena thought herself as a bird that could launch itself into the air and fly high in the sky to unknown places. She often watched the white and gray sea eagles as they dipped and soared into the sky from her perch in the tree, wishing that she could join them.

Kalena crouched down and scrubbed her hands in the sand among the tree roots to enable her to get a better purchase on the trees rough bark. She dusted her hands on her chest as she stared up at first branch above her. Tucking her skirt into her waistband, Kalena jumped and swung up onto the first branch and began to climb. She had climbed this tree hundreds of times and knew the best way to her favorite branch. The hard bark felt reassuring under her hands and Kalena always loved the smell of the trees in springtime.

Agile as a cat, she climbed to near the top of the tree and stopped to rest finally on a large, thick branch that jutted out at an upright angle from the main trunk. Kalena straddled the branch and crept slowly along it until she was over half way along its length. From here, she had a clear view of the field below and of the village. Above her, she had the open sky.

Kalena felt the morning sun on her back and heard the soft sighing of the leaves as the breeze teased them. Lifting herself just enough to pull Kala from her waistband, Kalena arranged the doll to lie in front of her so that she could see the view as well.

"We can both pretend to be birds again," the girl said as she arranged Kala's arms so that they crossed behind the doll's head. "Or, if you don't want to do that, we could pretend that we are Princesses that have been kidnapped and hidden in a tower, waiting for someone to rescue us. Maybe even a Hatar Flyer could rescue us, I like the Hatar." Kalena had never seen a Hatar, but her father had and from his stories, she knew she would like them and they would like her. Plus they could fly, maybe even better than a bird. Kalena stared at the rag doll a moment.

"No, not that either?" Kalena snorted. "What do you want to do then?"

Movement in the village caught Kalena's eye, and she shifted her gaze from Kala to Kurst Village.

She could see people surrounding two men on horseback in the Town Square. At the far end of the square could be seen a box wagon with a team of two horses. Lounging on the seat were two men in uniform. Beside the wagon was the long trestle table that was brought out for special occasions such as Winter Night and Summer Night. Kalena did not know what the occasion was today but upon noticing the tables, she realized what her nose had been trying to tell her since coming to her tree; that cakes and sweets were being prepared.

Kalena could not make out faces but the uniforms proclaimed the riders as Provosts. Before them was a group of adults with a small cluster of children who clung to their parents. She could see that the men were in close conversation with Kurst Elder, her father and two others who she could not see properly. Kalena saw one of the horsemen frantically gesticulate and heard the man turn and call to one of the wagon guards.

She watched as her father rushed forward and grabbed the horseman's stirrup crying desperately for the man to stop. The horseman, Kalena could now see that his head was bald, turned in his saddle and lashed out at her father with a gauntleted fist.

Kalena let out a gasp as he fell to the ground. Kurst Elder bent to look at her father, not seeing the other horseman catch the back swing of the bald one before it could hit him in the head. Kalena clutched Kala tightly to her. She could not see her mother anywhere in the village crowd. Voices murmured angrily and the bald one roughly pulled his arm from the younger man's grasp. He then rose in his stirrups and spoke over the noise of the crowd. Kalena could not make out what he said, but the villagers quieted.

"There you are!" a voice said from below her.

Kalena looked down from her branch to see her brother Videan staring back at her. He was a tall gangly lad with short black hair and luminous blue eyes. Kalena had heard some of the other girls talking about him, saying how handsome he was. She always felt a stab of jealousy because Videan spent more time talking with the older girls than with her. Movement flashed in the corner of her eye. She turned her head and saw one of his friends dashing across the wheat field back to the village.

"A man just hit Father!" she called down to her brother.

"If he did, it's all your fault," Videan called back to her. His remaining friends quickly arranged themselves around the bottom of the tree, effectively blocking any chance of escape. Kalena stared at her brother and did not like the way Videan looked at her.

"Why is it my fault?" Kalena was on the point of sobbing.

"Because Father was giving you away today, and you weren't there," Videan said with what sounded like great satisfaction in his voice.

"You're lying. Father would never give me away. He loves me!"

Videan started to laugh and the boys around the tree echoed him.

"He loves me more. I am the eldest and you are Second Born. He cannot love something that belongs to someone else. He sent me out this morning to find you. He wanted you there on time for the Provost."

"The Provost! I haven't done anything wrong. I don't want to go to jail!"

"Stupid girl," Videan said more to himself than to those around him who laughed viscously at the comment.

"Get down here right now!"

"No, you're a mean, horrible brother. Go away and leave me alone." Kalena broke down in tears and held her rag doll close to her chest. "Kala says to leave me alone!"

"I don't give a toss about Kala," Videan called back to her, eyes filled with hate. He took to step forward when the snort of a horse stopped him.

The distant thunder of hooves brought everyone's attention back to the village. One of the horsemen was coming across the wheat field towards them, Videan's friend trotting along in the lead.

As the small group came closer, the horse abruptly slowed its stride, and the rider raised an arm in acknowledgement before stopping the beast near the tree. The horse was beautiful and Kalena never ceases to be amazed by the stallion's beauty. His coat was as black as charcoal and as shiny as satin, his mane, tail, socks and nose was as white as the purest snow. Too bad his temper wasn't.

Shatal was a war-horse to be admired, and he knew it. His rider, on the other hand, was the complete opposite. A tall man in his mid-twenties with golden locks and startling blue eyes set in a strikingly handsome face which had the girls of the village swooning whenever he walked by. His athletic body sat his horse well and was dressed in the uniform of the County Provost, the emblem of a tan bear embroidered on an emerald green surcoat.

Both man and animal acted with the same mind; obvious in the fact that Shatal acted as if he wore no bridle, but held his head imperiously high as he trotted over.

When both horse and rider stood sweating beneath her, Kalena scrambled to her knees on the branch and bowed in the deepest curtsy she could manage without falling from the Coastgum. The sight of the stallion made her forget her tears. She often wondered whether the horse knew how human he sometimes looked.

"Welcome, Provost Garrick Thurad."

A satisfied snort from Shatal brought color to her cheeks as she tried not to laugh at the horse.

Garrick was her best adult friend and never called her by her full name except on formal occasions. Kalena was old enough to be flattered that a man so handsome and so old would want to be her friend. Garrick would spend time with all the younger children, especially if they were a second child, but would always find extra time to be with her.

Kalena suddenly turned to look at her brother.

"Provost Thurad would never put me in jail!"

Videan only smiled at her.

"Who said anything about jail?" the Provost said.

"Videan said that you were taking me away from Mother and Father, that they didn't want me anymore." Kalena began to cry again.

"What rubbish, I am not going to put you in jail. Come down from that tree and return with me to the village." The Provost sat straight in his saddle as he watched her, his right hand gripped nervously at the hilt of the ceremonial blade that swung at his hip.

"I don't want to, I'm scared. That other man hit father." Kalena's face grew stubborn.

"He didn't mean to. Your father startled him that's all. I have to bring you back to the village." Garrick seemed to let his words hang mournfully in the wind and his blue eyes turned to stare blankly over the wheat field towards the village.

"Why?"

Kalena faltered when the expression on Garrick's face hardened as he looked up at her.

"Because you are needed." The Provost looked back again towards the village. Kalena followed his gaze and saw that the other man just sat his horse staring intently at them across the wheat field. The villagers surrounding him seemed uncertain about what to do and had started moving around nervously. Kurst Elder still tended her father who was now propped up against the stone well clutching his forehead. He looked to be all right.

"I want to stay here," she said. Her mother said she had a stubborn streak a mile wide, Kalena knew that you never disobeyed a Provost–even if he was your friend.

"No." He shook his head in emphasis, his blonde hair falling into his eyes.

"But I'm scared," Kalena said softly, Kala's head was wet with her tears.

"There is no need to be scared. I won't let anything happen to you." Garrick held out both arms motioning with them for her to come down.

"You promise?" Kalena looked uneasily at the circle of boys below her.

"I promise. I'll even let you ride Shatal back to the village. You like Shatal don't you?"

The promise of touching Shatal made Kalena quickly forget her tears.

"You really mean that?" she asked uncertainly. Garrick never lets any of the children touch his warhorse.

"Of course."

Kalena hesitated a moment, her stubbornness arguing in her head not to believe him. Mother had taught her to always obey a Provost, so she pushed that little voice away and climbed quickly down the tree. Kalena stopped before the final jump, looking uncertainly at the boys who still stood around the base of the oak. Videan seemed ready to leap upon her at any moment; there was the hint of violence in his eyes and that was what truly frightened her. She had never truly seen this side of her brother before.

Garrick sighed as his blue-eyed gaze swept the surrounding boys. The warhorse began to dance nervously, sensing his rider's frustration. The Provost solved Kalena's problem by nudging Shatal between the boys to stand beside the trunk just beneath her.

"Let me help you down, they won't hurt you." Garrick frowned down at the boys and they all, including Videan, took an involuntary step back.

Garrick held out his arms and Kalena allowed herself to be lifted from the trunk onto Garrick's saddle.

Kalena settled herself comfortably and set Kala in front of her so that she could see as well.

"Is that better?" Garrick asked her.

"Yes thank you," Kalena beamed a huge smile at him. "Kala says thank you as well."

The Provost nodded and wrapped a strong, muscular arm around her, taking Shatal's reins in his right hand. He then turned Shatal around and began walking him slowly back to the village.

As the horse walked out from under the oak, Kalena turned her head to look behind her under Garrick's arm. The group of boys was trailing slowly behind the horse and Kalena impetuously stuck her tongue out at them making a rude sound. The Provost looked down in surprise. This sparked a giggle from Kalena that Garrick soon couldn't resist and finally gave into. Garrick's laughter seemed to ease the set of his features, to make them gentle again.

Kalena turned forward again and held Kala

out before her on outstretched arms, giggling. She loved horses, and she had never been on one as fine as this. Shatal's white mane flashed in the morning sun and his head nodded up and down as if agreeing with her about how wonderful he was. Thoughts of horses quickly changed to thoughts on birds and then, halfway across the wheat field Kalena suddenly asked, "Have you ever seen Hatars Provost Thurad?"

Kalena felt the arm around her waist tighten as he answered carefully.

"Yes, I have."

"What are they like? Do they fly better than birds? I've always wanted to know. Did you know that Father has seen a Hatar?" Kalena quickly closed her mouth as the Provost held up a shushing finger.

"One question at a time."

"Stop annoying the Provost Kalena, you won't be seeing him again," Videan said from beside the horse. Kalena had not noticed his arrival.

"Be quiet about things that do not concern you Videan," Garrick said angrily to him.

Videan clamped his mouth shut but still walked close to Shatal's side.

"Do you like Hatars?" He asked Kalena in a gentler tone.

"If they fly as good as birds I do," she said excitedly. "Do they fly as good as birds?"

The Provost nodded.

"They fly better than birds, faster, higher, and longer," Garrick emphasized each point with the arm that was holding her in the saddle.

"Do they? Do you think I will ever see

one?" Kalena asked, bending her neck to look up at him.

"Sooner than you think."

He smiled as he tickled her with his rein hand and she giggled.

"When you are finished playing with that child?"

Suddenly the tickling stopped and Kalena looked into the eyes of the bald headed man. This close and she could see the close trimmed gray beard and the hard wrinkles around his eyes and mouth. He looked older than Kurst Elder! He had ridden out to meet them on the edge of the wheat field. His big gray gelding had stopped placidly beside them; Shatal snorted and bared his teeth but received no reaction from the gray. The boys had stopped just behind the two horses.

"Is this the child?"

Garrick looked down at her and smiled.

"Yes, High Provost Deten."

Kalena shrank back against Garrick's chest. She did not like the way those deep brown eyes looked at her. Holding her doll close, she tried to pretend that she wasn't there.

"A valuable prize," Deten said more to himself. "She is not to mix with the other Kalarthri. She is to ride with you." The gray gelding shifted under Deten as he spoke, shifted away from the stallion. "You have done good work Provost. They should send more Testers into the Provinces."

The High Provost circled around them and then heeled his horse into a trot back to the Village Square.

"I don't like him," Kalena said sourly.

"Not many people do," Garrick said quietly, for Kalena's ears only.

"Why is she so valuable?" Videan's voice piped up from beside them.

The Provost looked carefully at the boy, his arm tightening his grip around Kalena.

"She is to be a Hatar Kalar boy."

Videan's face fell in disbelief as Garrick heeled his horse to follow Deten's.

Kalena was concentrating hard at Deten's retreating back and did not hear Garrick's reply.

As Shatal entered the Town Square, Kalena tried to look over the heads of the villagers surrounding them to get a glimpse of her father. Videan and his friends melted into the crowd and disappeared.

"He's fine Kalena, I see the Elder helping

him into the Town Hall."

Kalena looked up into the Provost's face and hugged her doll closer to her. This day was not turning into what it was supposed to.

"Where's Mama?" Kalena asked quietly as she looked through the crowd again. The Provost didn't hear her. She had only just started to call her mother 'Mother'. Saying Mama seemed childish but Kalena began to feel scared again.

The bald man, Deten, was speaking to the people who crowded around him. The two men who were sitting on the wagon were now herding five children into the back of it. She saw the mothers of Tobe and June crying after their sons but the parents of the others were nowhere to be seen.

Kalena turned frantically in the saddle and began to tug at the Provost's surcoat.

"Where's Mama?" she cried, trying to get his attention.

Garrick did not notice. His attention was fully on his superior. The villagers had started to close around the two horsemen and Garrick nudged his horse closer to the gray.

"Listen to me!" the bald man shouted over the crowd. "We have a lot of places to visit before sundown. We cannot stay for your wake. Let us through."

"Mama!" Kalena called at the top of her lungs. Tears flowed freely down Kalena's face and soaked into Kala's head, which was tucked under her chin. A roughly callused hand reached across and brushed wet, black hair away from her face.

"Shush, it will be alright. Your Mama is fine."

Kalena looked silently into the Provost's face. The morning sun made his short blonde hair shine about his head like a halo and his eyes held unshed tears as he looked down at her.

"What about a goodbye for our children?" a voice called from the crowd. Kalena thought it was Goodwife Keane. Many voices shouted agreement.

High Provost Deten turned his gelding to face the bulk of the crowd. Provost Thurad continued his horse moving until they stood beside the box wagon. Kalena could see Tobe, June and Anna's faces jammed against the iron bars of the only window in the wagon. The Guards stood alertly by the front of the wagon, hands ready by the sheathed swords that hung from their belts.

"They are no longer your children; they are the property of the Emperor. Disobedience to him is death." The High Provost shouted this to the crowd who instantly quieted and backed quickly away from him.

"It's nice to see some respect for the Emperor," Deten said softly though every member of the crowd heard him clearly.

Several people looked anxiously at each other, afraid that any action they do would be taken as defiance against the Emperor.

Satisfied that the villagers would give him no more trouble, High Provost Deten signaled his men to ready the wagon to leave. Guiding his horse to stand next to Shatal, the man turned in the saddle to face the village.

"We will be back in another eight years. Maybe, this time will teach you not to mollycoddle your Second Born."

The two soldiers now sat on the high seat of the wagon, and the man holding the reins slapped them hard against the horse team when the High Provost gave the signal to leave.

"Mama!" Kalena desperately called again, "Mama." Garrick had lied to her. She did not want to go to jail.

The children from the wagon began to echo her call. Provost Thurad looked back sadly at the silent crowd before following the wagon out of the village.

Kalena looked back at the square and saw her brother Videan push to the front of the crowd and stand smiling like the cat that had the cream. Movement at the back of the crowd drew her eyes and Kalena saw her father stagger into the square closely followed by Kurst Elder. Blood still stained the front of his face.

"Papa!" she called. Kalena tried to wave to him but the Provost held her in a vice like grip and heeled his horse into a faster gait to catch up to the retreating wagon.

"Remember that ma and pa love you," Kalena heard her father call to her hoarsely.

"Let me go," Kalena said trying to pry his arm away from her. Garrick did not answer her but looked sternly ahead of them. She began to struggle, trying to pummel Garrick with her tiny fists. "Let me go," She repeated over and over.

The Provost did nothing as Shatal cantered over the small rise that hid them from the main village except to keep his vice like grip around Kalena's waist.

Kalena quickly gave up her struggle and

began to cry silently. Her friends in the wagon still called for their parents. She heard Anna's high-pitched screech and cringed as it sent shivers down her spine. Kalena hoped it had the same effect on the men around her.

The Provost cantered ahead of the wagon and bought Shatal to a walk as he came alongside the gray gelding.

Kalena tried not to look at the bald man sitting in the saddle beside them. She did not like the way his eyes looked at her.

Ahead of them on the road waited ten more uniformed men on horseback who rode forward towards the transport. As the group of horsemen approached, The High Provost called to the lead man.

"Captain, shut that lot up before they

damage themselves."

The Captain signaled too two men who then rode forward to bang hard on the sides of the wagon and warned the children in hard voices to be silent. The rest of the men waited until the wagon had passed before falling in behind it.

The group had traveled a good mile from the village before the High Provost spoke again.

"I can sense your disapproval Thurad," he said. Kalena had cried herself out and was now leaning quietly against the Provost's chest, hoping that the bald man would forget about her.

"They are children -." Garrick simply said but Wolde Deten clipped the end of his comment.

"They are Kalarthri. You seem to forget that."

"It makes no difference whether they are

Kalarthri or freemen; they are still children and should be treated as such." Garrick's voice held a restrained anger. Kalena was glad it was not directed at her.

"I now see why you were sent out to the Provinces. Your father could not keep your views at the Capital could he?"

"I suggest that you keep my father out of this," Garrick said softly and to Kalena's wonder, the wrinkled old man snapped his mouth shut in surprise. "Remember, to speak of my father with such familiarity is treason."

The man's face turned red and Kalena could not decide whether it was from anger or embarrassment. The pair rode silently for a while before the High Provost spoke again.

"I understand that Harada, your Kalarthri

brother has just made Wing Commander."

"*Prince* Harada achieved that under his own merit," Garrick replied defensively though also with a small amount of pride.

"Harada *Kalar* has done well for a Kalarthri, especially one so young," Deten emphasized the title.

"Harada is a Hatar rider. Not plain Kalarthri."

That comment sparked a memory in Kalena.

"A Hatar rider? That's what you said I was going to be," Kalena said aloud. "You also said that they fly better than birds." Kalena looked up to see those bright blue eyes staring down at her. Her earlier terror was suddenly forgotten, if she was to ride Hatars, then she could visit her parents anytime she wanted, and scare her brother to boot.

"That's right, I did." Garrick smiled down at her.

"Does your brother, Harada," Kalena stumbled over the unfamiliar name, "like being a Hatar rider?"

"Yes, he does. He has made a good friend in Samar. Perhaps you will find a good friend in the partner you are paired with."

"Does that mean I'm not going to jail?" Kalena asked unsure of the answer.

"No, you are not going to jail."

"You, my dear, are worth a lot to me. This will be the first Bounty paid to me in over fifteen years."

Provost Thurad snored with disgust. Kalena glared at the bald man, hoping her expression looked as stern as Provost Thurad's. She did not want to speak to the man. What is a bounty? Kalena did not want to ask in case the High Provost answered her. When she was a Hatar rider, she will seek out Garrick's brother and be friends with him; he surely would be as nice as Garrick is, even if Garrick was a Provost.

"Where are we going?" she asked after a moment.

"When we finish the last of our patrol, we will be heading for Darkon," Garrick said.

"There you and the others will be assessed to find out what you are suitable for," Deten said throwing Provost Thurad a dark look.

"You'll be fine," Garrick said hugging her closer to him, staring hard at Wolde Deten's back as he rode ahead. "You'll be fine."

The rest of the day was spent traveling the country roads in silence, not even the soldiers talked amongst themselves. The countryside looked the same as that around Kurst Village and the villages themselves were much smaller than her own. Kalena stayed with Provost Thurad and fell asleep in the saddle, dozing against his chest. They found no others like her. No other Kalarthri in the region had the simple spark in them for bonding with the Speaking Crystal. Without that spark, the implanted Crystal will bring death to both the human and the Hatar partner.

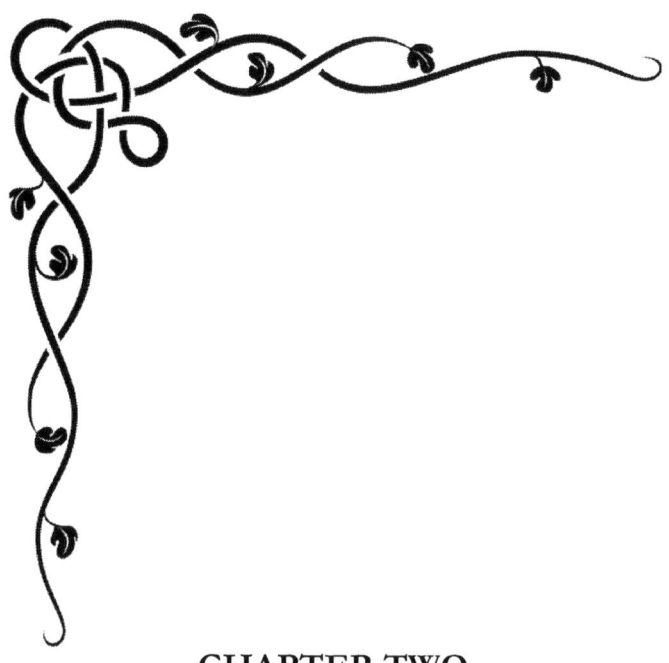

CHAPTER TWO

THE CHOOSING

Kalena awoke in her bed and found herself in the same, plain dormitory as what she fell asleep in. It was just before dawn and the five other children who shared the room with her were still asleep. Kalena hugged Kala and buried herself deep under her warm blankets.

She had been in this room for three weeks now and had been alone for the first week until Corey arrived. Another four children quickly followed Corey, and the dormitory did not seem quite so empty. They were allowed out of the dormitory for three hours each day into a grassed open-air enclosure in which they must exercise. The rest of the day was spent in a classroom, learning about the Suene Empire, its history and its armed forces. This was a new experience for Kalena as it was the first time that she had been in a classroom. The children of Kurst village were taught to read by their parents and enough mathematics to be able to make sure that they were getting the correct amount of money for their produce.

When Kalena was outside in the enclosure, she could sometimes hear the voices of other children and she often wondered what had happened to the others from her village. She had not seen them since the High Provost had brought them here to Darkon.

During the last three days in the classroom, they had been learning about the Hatar'le'margarten, the large feathered bird-like reptiles that are the core of the Suenese Flying Corps. And finally, their teacher Parker had introduced them to his wing mate, Fanta. Fanta was a large, sandy colored Hatar with large wings covered in golden feathers, but the rest of his body was covered in small, soft down feathers that rippled and moved over Fanta's muscled limbs.

Kalena hugged Kala close to her but did not

rush up to the Hatar like the rest of the children. She remained seated behind her desk, eyes glued to the reptilian head that towered above the group of excited children. Nictitating eyelids blinked over the sapphire slit eyes. As Kalena stared into Fanta's eyes she realized that she was being stared back at. She pulled herself straighter in her chair and jutted a defiant chin as she deliberately stared back at the Hatar.

The beak full of sharp teeth or the foot long claws that clicked loudly on the flagstone floor did not frighten Kalena. She just did not like being stared at. Kala did not like being stared at either.

'Parker, that little one is cocky. She will make a fine Wing Commander one day.'

The voice whispered on the edge of Kalena's awareness and she saw Parker look up at her and smile.

'She has a right to be cocky. Provost Thurad says that she is the strongest Gift he has ever seen.'

The reply whispered again on the edge of Kalena's awareness. Kalena felt the blood rise in her face. She did not like to be talked over.

"I am not cocky and I think you are both rude for talking as if I wasn't here!"

Kalena's childish anger was soothed a little by the look of shock that passed across Parker's face and Fanta stood stock still, his eyes fixed unblinkingly on Kalena and Kala.

After a moment, Parker shook himself and rose from his desk. Giving Fanta a knowing glance, he walked slowly over to Kalena and pulled out a chair to sit across the desk from her.

"Did you hear us speaking?" Parker asked carefully. He sat with the back of the chair against his chest, his chin resting on the top of the chair back.

"Of course I could," Kalena said with a little arrogance. *Parker must think that everyone is deaf.* Kalena placed Kala in a sitting position on the tabletop. "Kala did as well."

"Kala's the doll?" Parker asked uncertainly.

Kalena nodded. *Kala is more than a doll* but Kalena did not want to argue the point. She was beginning to feel a little uncomfortable under Parker's gaze. It was then that she noticed that the rest of the group had stopped touching the Hatar and was now watching her and their teacher.

'What do you think Fanta?'

'Speak to the Commander, she will need to

be tested further.'

"Tested further for what?" Kalena began to feel a sting of fear deep in her gut.

"You heard us again," Parker mumbled to himself.

"I want my mama." Kalena then broke into tears.

That afternoon Kalena was taken from her classroom to an open enclosure and placed in the center of a circle of Wingmen and their Hatar Partners. She was then told curtly by the Freeman Infantryman who escorted her to the gathering that she had to repeat aloud whatever she heard the Hatar Kalarthri say to each other. Kalena stood there in the center of the circle for nearly three hours repeating everything before a strange voice from outside the circle shouted, "Enough!"

Kalena was then rushed quickly back to her dormitory by the Infantrymen in time for dinner. She was left, bewildered and confused to eat dinner and go to bed. The other children avoided her as if she had caught the Plague.

The next morning Kalena did not feel she could face the coming day. She remembered the circle of Hatars and people from yesterday and shivered. The Hatars themselves had stood impassively around her, glittering like a jeweled rainbow in the afternoon sun. But their human wing mates…. Over the course of the testing, their faces slowly turned from annoyed boredom to outright horror as they realized that she could hear their every private thought.

Kalena hated being the focus of that horror. She was glad that the Freemen did not know that she could read their thoughts as well. She just did not choose to listen to their boring thoughts. Also, Kalena thought it a little rude to eavesdrop on someone while they are thinking.

She sat up in bed and hugged Kala to her. It was then Kalena realized that she was alone in the dormitory. The others had left without waking her for breakfast.

Tears began to trickle down her cheeks. Kalena seemed to have an endless supply of them and this snub by her dormitory mates broke her final straw. Kalena hugged Kala to her chin and the rag doll's worn face slowly soaked up the salty drops as they fell.

It was then that Kalena heard a soft whispering on the edge of her hearing and she lifted her head to try to hear it better.

The whispering stopped. Kalena crinkled her eyes in annoyance, now she was being whispered about.

"Hello. Is anyone there?"

Kalena pushed out of her blankets and crawled to the foot of her bed to have a better look through the main doors that lead out of the dormitory. She saw and heard nothing.

Backing away from the edge of the bed, she sat back on her feet, thinking. Kalena was sure that she heard something.

'Hello, little one.'

The masculine voice in her head made Kalena jump in surprise. Mindspeak, she had heard

Mindspeak right in her head.

'Why are you crying? We would like to know.'

'We.' The voice sounded a little distant to Kalena and as it spoke, she was sure that she could hear the whispering of others behind it.

'Because I'm scared and I want my Mama!' she replied. This is the first time she had actually spoken to someone with her mind without speaking the words aloud.

'You are the one that can hear Hatars and their Wing mates talk?'

Kalena's tears slowly began to stop flowing as she forgot about her fears. This person sounded nice.

'Yes, I can hear them. Can't everybody?'

Kalena heard some excited whisperings and

a female voice echoed quickly above the whisper.

'The four were right, the four were right!'

'Please, quiet.'

Kalena heard the male voice say, and she now knew that several other people were listening as well. Suspicion flared in her mind. What if this was another test?

'What's going on here?' she asked. Kalena heard the background-whispering drop to silence.

'We have heard that you will be joined to a Hatar earlier than expected,'

'Am I?' Kalena interrupted excitedly. That means she will know what it is to fly!

'Yes,' said the male voice patiently. *'And I have been chosen to be your partner. My name is Adhamhma'al'mearan. Humans call me Adhamh.'*

'Really, you're a Hatar?' Excitement ran

down Kalena's spine. Her tears were now completely forgotten.

'Yes, for I am like you. I can hear the other humans as they Mindspeak, though the humans do not know this.'

Kalena frowned at this.

'Do you mean that the others cannot hear me speak to you? They cannot hear you either?'

'Other humans will only hear me if I want them to,' Adhamh replied.

That was why they were all interested in her. That was why the soldiers that tested her yesterday did not like her. Because they now knew she could hear every private conversation, they spoke with their partners and know their every private thought.

Kalena shivered as she felt Adhamh quickly withdraw from her. How rude, she hadn't finished speaking with him yet!

Then suddenly he was back.

'I've just been told they are coming for us right now...'

'Who's coming for us?' Kalena interrupted but the Hatar ignored her. Adhamh just forced his voice over hers.

'Don't be afraid, we will meet soon enough in the flesh but remember one thing. Once the Krytal has been performed, pretend you can hear only my voice–do you understand?'

'Yes but...'

Then suddenly Adhamh's presence was gone from her, leaving Kalena sitting stunned on her bed. It was as her mind cleared that Kalena gradually heard the marching of booted feet on the flagstones as they came for her.

"Mama…" she said softly, hugging Kala to her.

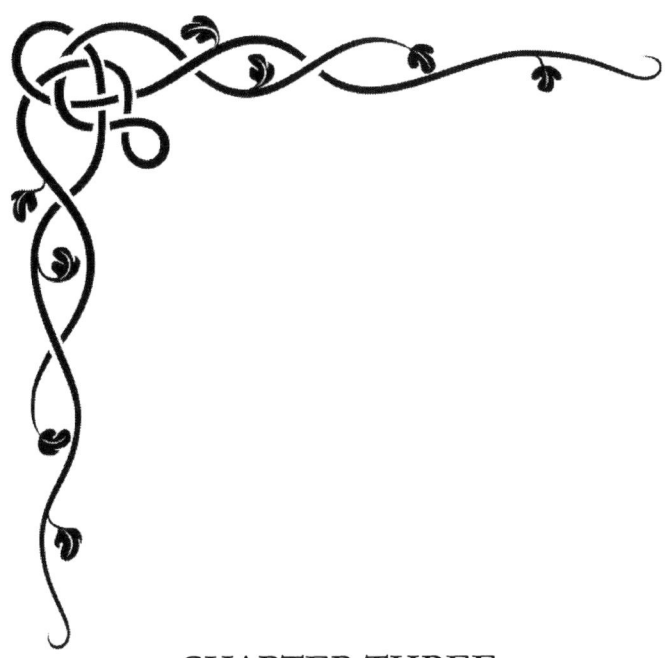

CHAPTER THREE

THE KRYTAL

Kalena stood quietly in between the two freeman infantrymen who had come to collect her. She held Kala close to her chest, afraid that the two men might take the doll from her. They had remained silent as they took Kalena from her bed and marched her out of the dormitory enclosure into the rabbit warren that was Darkon.

As Kalena walked, her eyes zoomed everywhere. It was dark, the day she had arrived here with the Provosts and she had seen nothing of her surrounds before going into the dormitory enclosure. But now she could see the outside.

Scattered around the area were several more enclosures like the one Kalena had just left. Some were small like hers; others were larger. The enclosures arced away in either direction, skirting the central buildings and grounds. Even now as she walked quickly past them Kalena could hear the sounds of children's voices. But of the people outside the enclosures, she was the only child. Everyone was either an adult in uniform or a Hatar and Kalena dared not speak to either after Adhamh's warning.

As they passed Hatar Kalar, Kalena could hear the faint whisperings of their mind speech. But she kept her thoughts forwards and ignored them. She was very glad that her escort was freemen. They cannot speak with their minds–at least Kalena hadn't met one who could. And private thoughts are easy to screen out from her mind's ears, it is something Kalena instinctively did otherwise her head would be continually full of noise and chatter.

Even with all her gawping, Kalena was virtually made to trot to keep up with the two infantrymen. They did not seem to realize that she had shorter legs than they did. The men looked gruff and unfriendly otherwise Kalena would have complained. But concentrating on keeping her feet moving fast enough to keep up took Kalena's mind off what lay ahead–The Krytal.

Adhamh sounded as if he did not like this thing much. Actually, Kalena thought he sounded a little frightened. Kalena's thoughts would run this far before one of the soldiers would place a rough hand on her shoulder to hurry her along. Distracted, she would then forget her chain of thought and start them all over again.

Kalena made no effort to speak to the soldiers, and they made no effort to even acknowledge her, moving her along as a butcher would lead an animal to the block.

The three made their way out of the ring of the Kalarthri enclosures and entered the central administration area of Darkon. Most of the buildings were large, one storey affairs with neat signs hanging above their main entrances telling outsiders what its duties were or the building's purpose. Interspersed between these buildings were large rectangular open areas, some grassed some not, where freeborn infantry and cavalry men were lining up for the morning parades and drills. The green grass contrasted strongly with the rusty color of the bare earth.

It was the first time that Kalena had seen firsthand the many different uniforms that they had been taught in the classroom.

They passed through the parade grounds and finally turned off the main thoroughfare towards a large building with a large sign above the door that Kalena could not read. On either side of the door stood two armed Infantrymen who swept the three of them with a glance before deciding to ignore them.

Kalena was then ushered down several

corridors before being marched through a set of large double doors that opened into a gigantic hall, the sight of which stopped Kalena in her tracks.

Everything was painted white, including the stone floor and the wooden benches that lined the walls. The dark uniforms of the people that occupied these benches stood out like a beacon against the white of the hall. The hall was filled with the murmuring of people. There were a lot of uniforms lining the benches and Kalena's recent education told her that these are high ranking freemen. It was then that Kalena realized that she had not seen any Kalarthri soldiers on her way through the inner ring and there were none in the hall.

A rough hand on the back of her neck bought Kalena's attention back to the Infantrymen standing next to her. Keeping his hand where it was, the man left his companion to lead Kalena into the center of the hall.

Kalena did not resist him but the sight of all those eyes upon her made Kalena extremely self-conscious. They stopped before a large white block made of a material Kalena did not recognize and the murmuring of the uniforms around her instantly stopped.

The hall now sat in silence and it was now that Kalena noticed the two men who stood on the other side of the white block. They were dressed completely in white, from the leather of their boots to their rough woolen tunics, vests and trousers. They both wore their hair and beards long and had them intricately braided with bells that tinkled and flashed as they talked quietly together. One of the men held a small plain wooden box carefully in his hands as if the slightest movement could destroy it.

A man rose from the bench closest to them and his boots echoed through the quiet hall as he walked towards them.

The infantryman immediately removed his hand from Kalena's neck to thump a salute onto his chest. Kalena rubbed a hand over the back of her neck. The soldier's fingers had hurt, but she kept an eye on the man who had approached them. He did not look very friendly.

"Captain Jerant Sir," the Infantryman spouted as the Captain stopped smartly before them.

"This is the girl then?" The Captain asked without any pleasantries.

"Yes, Sir."

The Captain stood silently a moment and

looked at her, making Kalena feel like a horse for sale at a market. In response, Kalena stared back at him like she did to the Hatar, Fanta. Kalena made sure that Kala started hard at him as well.

Captain Jerant was tall and thin and his uniform hung loosely about him but was pressed and neat. His peppered hair and beard were cut short and his brown eyes stared out from under thick bushy brows and seemed to miss nothing.

Kalena's courage began to fail under the Captain's sterile gaze and she made an involuntary step backwards to stand behind the soldier with her. Kalena relaxed when she was out of the Captain's full gaze and used the shielding of the soldier's back to poke her tongue at the Captain. She did not like him.

Captain Jerant turned his impassive face

away from Kalena and turned to look to the far side of the hall where two huge entry doors were being opened. At the first creak, Kalena poked her head out from behind the Infantryman's back to see what was happening.

The large doors opened to admit two rather large infantrymen who paused and gave a curt salute to the Captain before moving aside for those coming behind them.

Slowly stepping out from the darkness of the outer corridor came a large black Hatar, his black glossy wings held close to his back so as not to hit the entry door. The black feathers glinted green and blue as they caught the light from around the hall. The Hatar's underbelly was such a vivid blue that it reminded Kalena of a clear spring sky. His eyes were also a vivid blue with slitted black pupils that reminded Kalena of cats' eyes.

The soldiers lead the Hatar to the center of the hall, stopping on the other side of the white stone from Kalena. The Captain moved forward to meet them and he exchanged a few curt words with one of the infantrymen before running his gaze over the Hatar.

Since Captain Jerant had his attention focused elsewhere, Kalena stepped out from behind the solider and tried to look past the stone and surrounding people to get a good look at the Hatar. Kalena thought him the finest creature she had ever seen. Tucking Kala into the belt of her skirt, Kalena started to creep forward to get a better look but in a quick motion, she felt the soldier's hand on her neck again.

"Stay where you are," he said quietly. "You

will get your view of the beast soon enough."

Kalena glanced up at him, saw the man's stony countenance and decided against making a run for it. She could even vaguely imagine the spanking she would get for doing so.

It was then that the Captain looked away from the Hatar and turned to the two men in white. Giving them a respectful bow he said in ritualistic tones, "Let us begin for we are glad that the Pydarki has consented to release their charge into our care. We are humble in our gratitude and hope are most deserving of your gift."

To Kalena, the Captain looked anything but humble and the man in white not holding the box moved uncomfortably on his feet.

'The Ritual of Giving is old–the Pydarki are uncomfortable because they are as much slaves to

the Suene Empire as we are. Their 'Gift' is not given freely–but the words of the old ritual still remain. They have also argued against implanting the crystal in one so young but they have been forced into this.'

The sound of Adhamh's voice in her head made her jump in surprise and it was only the increased pressure of the soldier's hand on her neck that stopped her from replying to him.

Kalena looked around the room and saw the Hatar looking at her. That must be Adhamh!

Both the Pydarki gave Captain Jerant a deep bow in return, a bow that they retained until the Captain had seated himself with the rest of the uniforms. The two men then approached the white stone block.

Carefully, the man not carrying the box

touched the stone with the tips of his fingers, caressing it as he would the finest silk cloth. Slowly, as if due to the Pydarki's attention, the white stone itself began to glow.

Kalena stared at the block in wonder, excited beyond belief that she was here to see the stone glow. Any fear she harbored now was quickly forgotten as the stone's light bathed her face in warmth and comfort.

The Pydarki stepped back from the stone with a reverential bow and quickly gestured to the soldiers on either side of the stone.

His hand still tight on the back of her neck, the solider pushed Kalena forward. She saw that the two soldiers on the other side did the same with Adhamh. Both of them were being led to the two Pydarki, the tinkling of their braid bells now drowned out by the sounds of booted feet and the scrape of Adhamh's claws against the floor. The uniforms seated around them remained silent.

The soldier halted Kalena before the stone and on the other side, Kalena saw Adhamh's head rear up from the light. They stood staring at each other bathed in the light from the stone. It was the first time they had really seen one another.

"Place her on the Pyter," the man in white said.

The soldier nodded and without warning grabbed Kalena around the waist and heaved her onto the top of the white stone. Kalena cried out in terror, afraid that the glowing stone might burn her, but as her legs and hands came in contact with its surface, she was pleasantly surprised. It felt very soft and warm, rather like a goat bladder that had been filled with water.

"Look, Kala, it isn't hot." Kalena tugged at the head of the doll tucked into her belt, turning it to look at the stone through stitched eyes.

"Infantryman, please ensure that the child is secure." The Pydarki said as he slowly approached Adhamh, not looking back to see his request carried out.

The soldier gave the Pydarki no response but immediately gestured for Kalena to lie down on top of the stone. Kalena did not argue with him, she welcomed the full body warmth the stone gave her. She made herself comfortable on the stone, adjusting Kala in her belt so that the doll would not be crushed.

Once comfortable Kalena now noticed that the two soldiers that entered the hall with Adhamh had joined them. Each man then pulled a long strip of plaited leather from their belts and twisted it into large loops.

Suddenly two men reached out and grabbed an arm each and slipped their plaited loops around each of her wrists, the third man pulled her legs together and looped his cord around her ankles. Quickly, the soldiers pulled the bonds tightly and secured them somehow to the stone.

Kalena strained against her bonds but all she succeeded in doing was to cut the circulation in her hands and feet. The bonds were too tight. There was only one thing that she could think of to do. Kalena began to cry.

The soldiers moved away from her and disappeared from her field of vision. Tied now, all Kalena could see through her tear soaked eyes were the Hatar Adhamh to her left, the darkness of the ceiling above her and the emptiness of the hall to her right. She could no longer see the door that she entered through.

'Please, do not cry.'

Kalena heard Adhamh's voice again in her head. She immediately stopped her crying to listen to him.

'The bonds are necessary, do not fight them,' the Hatar continued once Kalena had calmed. *'Watch what happens to me and do not be afraid. Do as I do. When it is your turn, I will help you as I can.'*

'What is happening?' Kalena could not help replying. There were no Hatars or riders here to witness.

'The Pydarki is going to perform the Krytal.

First on me and then on you. Kalena, you must be brave and you must be strong.'

'They've tied me down!' Kalena cried mentally.

'That is for your own protection Kalena. Humans react differently to The Krytal than we Hatar'le'margarten. Just watch what happens to me.'

Kalena craned her head into a position where she could see Adhamh. The Hatar's black head was cocked to one side, his sapphire eyes staring intently at her. The sight of a carnivorous reptile staring at you like that would normally put the fear of The One into you, but to Kalena it was comforting. She did not feel scared anymore.

Then the Pydarki moved between them, breaking Kalena's line of sight with Adhamh. The man in white bowed slightly to the Hatar before signaling to his companion to join him. The man came into Kalena's field of vision, hands held tightly around the wooden box he carried. The first Pydarki then spoke to Adhamh, but it was so low that Kalena could not hear it. Adhamh gave no answer except to lower his head until it was level with the man's waist.

It was at this moment that the man holding the box began to hum. The sound was low and deep and Kalena realized that she felt the sound rather than heard it. It felt as if it traveled through the very rock itself. Kalena stared at the man in awe. She wished that she could do that!

The Pydarki then turned to the one with the box and carefully unlatched it, lifting the hinged lid until it rested on the humming man's chest. From

Kalena's angle, she could not see its contents. The man stood still a moment before reaching into the box and removed a small, delicate knife. It looked very sharp as it glinted in the light of the hall. Kalena looked on with renewed interest. What was the knife for?

In a tinkle of bells, the Pydarki then turned from the box and took a small step to stand just behind Adhamh's ear. Now that the man had moved, Kalena could see everything.

Again, the man spoke to the Hatar. Again Kalena could not hear what was being said. Adhamh remained stock-still. Taking the Hatar's stillness for an answer the Pydarki nodded to himself before leaning forward with the knife and quickly cutting a small incision behind what Kalena thought to be Adhamh's ear.

Kalena gasped at the sight. Adhamh did not even twitch and even now she could see the red of the Hatar's blood beginning to well and drip from the wound. It was not a very big cut; about the size of a man's thumbnail but it was enough to make Kalena uneasy.

The man then placed the knife back into the box and pulled out something else. The Pydarki held the object between his thumb and forefinger and showed it to Adhamh. The object glittered like a rainbow of many colors and seemed to pulse with its own inner light. It was beautiful and Kalena thought she could hear it singing to her.

The Pydarki then held it high for the hall to see and Kalena could now see that it was a faceted stone that drew the light from the hall and turned it into rainbows. Kalena heard the disquieted murmuring from the audience.

'Uniforms obviously do not appreciate beautiful things,' she thought to herself.

"Witness and Remember," the Pydarki said as he bought the stone down and held it gently against the new incision behind Adhamh's ear. Kalena tried to crane her head forward to get a better view. Blood washed over the stone, cutting off its rainbow light from the hall and Kalena could no longer hear its silent singing. She groaned in the loss and the Pydarki carrying the box looked curiously at her.

Then suddenly a red glow appeared where the stone was that grew in intensity as all the welling blood became absorbed into the stone. The Pydarki quickly released his grip on the stone as it began to sink into the incision, taking the eerie red glow with it. Within the blink of an eye, the stone was gone, buried inside the flesh next to Adhamh's ear. There was no sign of the cut and the Pydarki holding the box stopped his humming. The only reaction Adhamh had given to this violent intrusion was a slight curling of his upper lip. The Hatar then blinked three sets of eyelids before raising his head to its normal position.

Even now she could feel a tingling behind the flesh of her ear as Adhamh's words came back to her.

'...first on me and then on you...'

Kalena turned uneasy eyes to the Pydarki who were now moving towards her. What she could see of their faces behind their beards looked compassionate and kind. It did not look as if it had hurt Adhamh; maybe it just looks worse than it is.

'Adhamh, how do you feel?' She asked, looking for reassurance, but the Hatar gave no reply. Instead, he sat back on his haunches, shaking his head as if trying to shoo a fly.

Then her vision of Adhamh was blocked by the chest of the Pydarki. He stared down at her with ice-blue eyes, knowing that Kalena had seen what had happened to Adhamh. Gently, he placed a hand on her forehead and smoothed back her hair.

"My name is Asnar, my friend is called Angrave." The Pydarki spoke softly, just on the edge of her hearing. "We do not mean you any harm. The Speaking Crystal does not mean you any harm. We are about to perform the Krytal on you. Traditionally we would ask your consent to do this but under the Dominion of the Suene Empire, free will is not possible. Do you understand?"

The man looked down at her, the bells in his braids tinkling as they settled around him. He has no choice in the matter, but he still treated her like he would an adult. Kalena slowly nodded her head.

Asnar smiled down at her and said, "Be brave."

Kalena closed her eyes tightly and turned her head. She did not wish to see what was happening to her. A moment later she heard Angrave begin to a hum and then felt the nick of the blade behind her ear and could feel the trickle of blood run down into her hair. Oddly she did not feel any pain. The warmth of the stone seemed to drain it away from her. She then heard the sound of the speaking crystal being removed from the box and braced herself. Kalena felt the stone being passed in front of her closed eyes, felt it sing to her in greeting, then she heard Asnar exclaim, "Witness and Remember." She then felt a nudging behind her ear and Kalena tensed.

Curiously, Kalena felt nothing at first and then suddenly it felt as if someone was poking at her behind her ear. It then became hot, it felt as if a burning coal was being held against her skin and Kalena began to squirm against her bonds. Then, somehow, she felt something move through her flesh growing tentacles in all directions from the space just behind her ear. The growth was quick and Kalena began to panic as she felt it touch the bones in her neck. She began to involuntarily thrash against her bonds as if someone else had control of her limbs. Kalena began to shake her head as if the thing could be tossed out with the force. But it did not work, Kalena could still feel it moving towards her brain.   Fear washed over her as the first tentacle moved into her nervous system.

Then Kalena fell unconscious.

CHAPTER FOUR

KALENA KALAR

Kalena awoke with a blinding headache and a burning sensation on her cheek. She immediately closed her eyes again as the light made the ache in her head pound worse. Around her, Kalena could hear nothing and the air felt cool against her skin. It felt like night time, but why was it so bright?

Kalena lay a moment in silence, her eyes tightly closed, slowly sensing the world around her. The feel and weight of cloth on her skin told Kalena that she was clothed and in a bed and she could feel the form of Kala tucked into the crook of one arm. Over her was a thin blanket, a corner of which she must have kicked off in her sleep, as Kalena could not feel it on her right foot.

Bracing herself, Kalena was determined to open her eyes, curious to find out where she was. This place did not feel like the dormitory, it was too quiet.

'Kalena?'

'Adhamh!' The sound of the Hatar's voice cheered Kalena no end. But Adhamh's mind voice was very faint and Kalena found it hard to

concentrate on it with her headache pounding away to her heartbeat.

'Yes, it is me. Do you remember my warning?'

Kalena did not need to think hard to remember what Adhamh had told her.

'Not to tell anyone that I can still hear other Hatars and their riders talking.'

'Good. Please remember that Kalena, both our lives now depend on both of us keeping this secret.'

'Can we still hear others after what…after those things were put into us?' Kalena imagined she could feel the bump that should be behind her ear.

'I can still hear the conversations that other humans have with their Hatar partners. I see no

reason why you should not either.'

"Good," Kalena said aloud in satisfaction.

"Kalena Tsarland, are you awake?"

A male voice that was deep and friendly sounded about the room.

'Adhamh, someone is here with me. I accidentally spoke aloud, and he heard me.'

'We will speak again later,' and then Adhamh was gone.

She heard someone move near to her. They had been sitting in a chair next to her all this time.

"Kalena, can you hear me?"

The man's voice became very insistent and Kalena held her eyes shut a few moments longer as she decided whether to feign sleep or not. But she cannot pretend to sleep forever and the headache Kalena felt upon waking was not as bad as it was.

The ache seemed to ebb slowly away with each thump of her heart. She slowly opened her eyes.

Kalena found that she was in a small room that contained the bed she was lying in, a couple of ladder-backed chairs, a clothes chest against the far wall and a small writing desk. It was all very cozy. The man standing next to her was another thing altogether.

He was much older than Kalena, at least in his early twenties. His thatch of thick brown hair stood out at odd angles from his head and he regarded her through dark brown eyes. On his left cheek was the small tattoo of a leaping ram. The man's uniform was one that Kalena recognized from her classroom. It was a Wing Lieutenants uniform, and it settled perfectly around his lean frame. The Blue and Red of his uniform collar proclaimed him to be from First Wing, Second Flight–the second best flying squadron in the Suene Empire. First Flight is the elite of the Flying Corps and is based in Hered, Suene's Capital–That much Kalena remembered from her lessons.

"How are you feeling?" the man asked giving Kalena a smile of reassurance as he seated himself in the chair that stood beside her bed.

Kalena sat up slowly in her bed, giving the area behind her ear a slight rub. As her fingertips brushed the skin, she could feel no trace of the knife cut or the Speaking Crystal. Kalena hugged Kala to her before giving the man a non-committal shrug.

"Who are you?" Kalena asked in an effort to ignore his question. She did not want to talk to this man about how she was feeling. Kalena wanted to find out more about what was going on, and she wanted to discuss things more with Adhamh. She desperately wanted to find out more about the Hatar. Apart from Kala, Kalena considered Adhamh her only friend in this place.

The man did not look to be shocked by her question. He seemed to be expecting it.

"My name is Gwidion Bessal, Second Lieutenant of First Wing, Second Flight. And I know that you are Kalena Tsarland who has just been accepted by The Krytal and is now linked with Adhamhma'al'mearan."

"Linked?"

"The Speaking Crystal gives you the power to speak to your Hatar partner through telepathy or mind-speak. I know you have experienced this so you know what I mean by it. Usually, humans cannot talk to Hatars with their minds but the

Speaking Crystals make this possible. We call it being 'linked', as the Crystals that are given to each partner are actually two halves of one entity. They have to be or the link will not work."

"What do you mean by being half of one entity?" Kalena asked, a little confused by Gwidion's explanation.

"I don't really understand it properly myself. The Pydarki are the ones to ask about that but do not expect them to answer you. What I just told you is what they've been telling us for the last hundred years."

"Oh." Kalena felt a little let down. This was the first time she had met an adult who admitted that they did not know everything. Then a question came to her.

"Who are the Pydarki?"

"That is hard to explain." Gwidion sat a moment in thought. "They are a people who live in the Bhaglier Mountains to the north of here. They are a secretive lot, full of ritual and mystery and though they come under the same laws as the rest of the Empire they remain oddly independent. Don't ask me why, I know not, but they do possess the secret of the Speaking Crystal and they are the only ones who are able to conduct The Krytal. That is all I can tell you."

Kalena raised her hand to scrub at the burning feeling on her left cheek but froze as Gwidion leaned quickly forward shaking his hands.

"Don't rub at it. Rubbing just makes it worse."

"Makes what worse?" Kalena's hand did not move as she spoke. It stayed hovering in the no-man's-land between the blankets and her face.

"While you were unconscious, the Administrators gave you a tattoo to mark who you are. It is exactly like mine." Gwidion pointed to the black inked leaping ram on his cheek. "All Kalarthri get one, though you probably haven't seen enough of us to know that."

"Really, I have a tattoo?" Kalena's voice filled with excitement as she looked down at Kala. "You will have to give Kala one too. See, there is a clean spot on her cheek where it could go."

"I will ask our best tattooist to paint one on for you," Gwidion could not help but smile as he spoke.

Then another question came to Kalena. This Gwidion Bessal seemed open to her questions, so she pushed ahead, asking without fear.

"Why was I picked to be a Flyer?"

"Candidates are chosen from the other Kalarthri due to their 'special talents'. Most don't even know they had talents. I didn't, anyway. Some people are born with the capacity to be able to use their mind to communicate, but they are unable to. Apparently, human minds are not built to be able to do this. That is why we use the Speaking Crystals. They become the conduits for our special human minds to communicate to its partner Crystal and then on to its Hatar host. As you can tell, Hatars can only communicate via telepathy so they need the Crystal to talk to us. Understand?"

Kalena nodded. This was something that she would have to talk to Adhamh about later. She felt sure that he said earlier that Hatar could talk to any human–not just gifted ones.

Gwidion paused a moment as if considering his next words.

"This was the generally accepted theory until you came along."

Kalena held her breath in fear–what were they going to do to her now?

The Lieutenant just sat there staring at her, though his eyes did not show fear like those other Flyers. If Kalena did not know better, she thought they held pity.

Then suddenly he stood from his chair muttering quickly to himself, "People will always be afraid of the unknown."

Kalena automatically huddled back in her bed at his abrupt movement, scared that he will grab her for something worst to come.

Realizing that his actions had been

misinterpreted he calmed himself.

"Don't worry. Nothing else is going to happen to you." The Lieutenant then held out his hand. "Take my hand and I will take you to meet the rest of the wing–after all, now you are one of them."

"Huh?" Kalena came out of her huddle, startled by what she had just heard.

"Come, the wing is in the Mess Hall eating dinner and you must be starving." A loud rumble from Kalena's belly confirmed him. "Wing Commander Thurad wants to introduce you to them. You are now a junior Wingman in First Wing, Second Flight. Training proper begins tomorrow."

Gwidion opened the door and Kalena moved uncertainly from the bed, Kala hugged tightly to her chest. She gingerly let her feet touch the floor and saw that her boots were placed neatly beside the bed. As Kalena pulled them on she found that her headache had now receded to a dull ache, and the light no longer felt like small needles being pushed into her eyes. She stood up and grabbed her jacket from the back of the chair that the Wing Lieutenant was sitting on and threaded her arms through the sleeves as she walked through the door.

The corridor outside was wide and uncluttered with torch brackets spaced evenly along the smooth stone wall.

"Come, the Mess Hall is this way."

Gwidion placed a gentle hand on her shoulder and guided her down the corridor. They had only walked a few steps when three men appeared from around the corner and came marching towards them. Kalena felt her heart flutter and nearly stop when she saw the gaunt figure of Captain Jerant between two infantrymen.

"Wing Lieutenant. Where do you think you are going with that girl?" the Captain's voice was hard and emotionless and Kalena moved closer to Gwidion. She did not like this man.

Gwidion snapped his feet together and made the Captain a small bow. "We are heading for the Mess Hall Sir."

The Captain stared at them a long moment.

"Has she been tested yet?" he suddenly asked.

"No Sir. Not properly."

"Do you think it wise to let her near other Hatar Kalar until you are sure she cannot hear them?"

Kalena felt the hand on her shoulder stiffen.

She clung tighter to the Wing Lieutenant.

"Test her for me now Kalar."

"What? She has only just undergone the Krytal."

"Talk to your beast now and let us see if she can hear you!" The Captain said leaving no room for argument.

Gwidion opened his mouth to say more but thought better of it.

"Very well."

He looked down at Kalena and she could not help but smile up at him.

"Kalena, I'm about to talk in mind voice. If you can hear me, can you repeat it for the Captain."

Kalena nodded as Adhamh's voice flooded through her head.

'Remember. Pretend you do not hear them.'

'I remember Adhamh.'

Gwidion eyes remained on her but they suddenly unfocused and Kalena heard the familiar whisperings in her mind.

'Kalena, if you can hear this tell the Captain that he is a fart faced maggot off of a horses rear that needs-'

'Gwidion! Be respectful.' A female voice said sternly.

'Sorry, Jolar but he is.'

Kalena tried not to show any reaction on her face. If she had said what Gwidion had said her father would have washed her mouth out with lye soap.

"Well?"

The Captain's voice cut through Gwidion's mental chatter. Kalena shrank back behind

Gwidion.

"Kalena, did you hear anything? I did not hear you repeat my words."

Suddenly she felt her arm gripped by fingers of iron and yanked forward and Kalena found herself face to face with the Captain. His thoughts were jumbled and confused but full of anger and fear. Kalena immediately blocked them from her mind.

"Answer the lieutenant Kalar."

Tears started to trickle down her cheeks and Kalena tried to stop herself from blubbering. Dimly a roar was heard from outside and she heard Gwidion talking urgently with the Captain.

"-you are upsetting her and her new Hatar partner. He feels her fear through the link."

The Captain seemed not to hear the

Lieutenant's words.

"Did you hear him?"

Kalena shook her head; her voice did not want to work.

Suddenly the Captain backhanded her across the face. She would have collapsed if not for the Captain's iron grip on her arm. Her face stung like fire and she felt Gwidion shift behind her.

"Answer me in an appropriate manner, Kalar."

"Damaging State property is not setting a good example for the men Captain Jerant."

The Captain released his grip and spun around in surprise. The two infantrymen immediately turned and smartly saluted. Kalena jumped back to Gwidion's side, and she felt him place a protective hand on her shoulder as he guided her back behind him.

"Provost Marshal Brock," the Captain stammered.

The Provost Marshall's eyes flicked across everyone present in the hallway, lingering longest on the red mark that now rose across Kalena's face.

"I think you need to come to my office and explain your actions to me, Captain. You know there is a ban on children undergoing the Krytal."

The Provost Marshall then swept past them and continued along the corridor without waiting to see if his request would be followed. Captain Jerant stood a moment glaring hard at both Kalena and Gwidion before turning swiftly to follow the Provost Marshall, the two Infantrymen following in his wake leaving the two Kalarthri standing alone in the corridor.

Gwidion suddenly laughed out loud.

"What a piece of luck. Provost Marshal Brock has an uncanny sense of timing. He was not supposed to be back at Darkon for another two days." Gwidion smiled down at her, "The Provost Marshall will put the Captain in his place. But come, the Wing Commander is waiting to meet you and we best not keep him waiting."

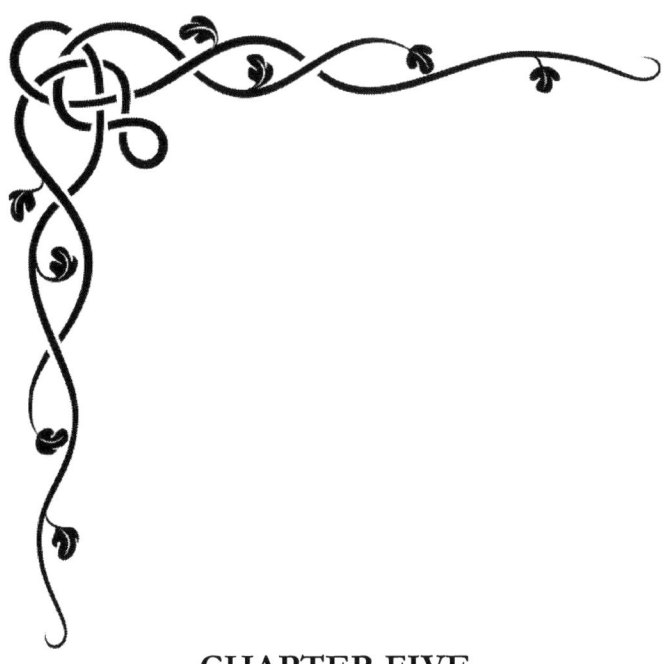

CHAPTER FIVE

HARADA THURAD

The Mess Hall was the largest room Kalena had ever seen. It could easily have contained all of the buildings that made up Kurst village with plenty of room to spare. The entire hall arched up to what she assumed was a rounded ceiling above her because at the moment the rafters were shrouded in a darkness created by the smoking torches that ringed the walls. The hall must be created out of one of the domed structures that Kalena saw this morning as she walked through Darkon with the two Infantrymen.

The room was filled with trestle tables and benches and most of them were crammed full of people eating and drinking and full of smiles and laughter. On the far side of the hall, Kalena saw a long counter with large pots and platters heaped upon it where people could go and serve themselves. The sight of the food made Kalena's stomach rumble again. She glanced up at Gwidion who stood next to her in the entranceway.

"Kalena, this is the Mess Hall where all the Hatar Kalar based at Darkon take their meals. The corridors behind us lead to our living areas with a rear door access to the barracks where the Hatar live.

"Where do the Hatar take their meals? Do they eat here as well? I can't see any here." Kalena looked around the hall just in case she had missed a large feathered form crouching among the tables. At the sound of choked laughter, she glanced sharply up at the Wing Lieutenant, unsure whether she was being made fun of. Kalena pushed Kala closer into the crook of her arm.

"The Hatar do not eat with us Kalena. For one thing, they are too large to have them all eat in a hall. For another, watching them eat live food can really put you off your dinner," Gwidion grinned down at her.

"Come, let us go and find the Wing

Commander and see what he makes of you. You are the youngest cadet we've ever had join the Wings."

Gwidion placed a firm hand on Kalena's shoulder and shepherded her into the crowd of tables and benches. As Kalena passed by she saw and smelt the food and hot drink that was being consumed by the Flyers at their tables. Her stomach grumbled in protest at being so sorely neglected. Kalena brushed her fingers across Kala's linen stomach.

"Kala, I see your stomach is rumbling too," Kalena said to the doll that stared back at her through the folds of her shirtsleeve.

"Gwidion, can we please get something to eat first? Me and Kala haven't had anything to eat at all today and we're starving." Kalena clutched dramatically at her stomach and groaned to emphasize her point. It was a trick that always worked on Mama.

"Yes all right. I'm feeling a little peckish myself."

Gwidion changed direction and weaved her through the warren of tables until they tumbled out near the food counter. Without waiting for the Wing Lieutenant Kalena rushed forwards and grabbed a plate and spoon from the stack and rushed along to the first pot only to find that she was too short to reach into it.

"This could be a bit of a problem," Gwidion said from behind her. "We can't have a Flyer not able to serve themselves," he said as Kalena and Kala swiveled around guiltily to look at him.

"We didn't mean to push ahead of you," she

said hoping that he was not too angry with her.

"No, that's all right. A hungry belly will make you do that. People are always hungry after going through the Krytal." Gwidion moved closer to the counter and quickly glanced at it, making a quick inventory of what was on offer.

"Here, give me your plate and I'll dish you out a healthy portion." Gwidion snatched the plate from her hands before she could complain and started along the table, dipping the spoon in and out of pots and platters heaping large amounts on both her plate and his own.

Kalena followed Gwidion to the end of the counter and quickly found herself suddenly carrying two thick slabs of crusty bread spread heavily with butter as the Wing Lieutenant juggled two full plates with spoons between his hands with another slice of bread stuffed into his mouth.

"Comfrhamh," Gwidion mumbled jerking his head towards the crowd to emphasize whatever directions came out of his mouth.

Kalena nodded back to him. She did not understand what he just said but the gist of it was clear. Taking a large mouthful of buttered bread, Kalena followed the Wing Lieutenant back into the buzzing mass of humanity that flowed thick amongst the trestle tables.

Kalena followed as Gwidion wove his way expertly through the crowds. Around her people were eating and drinking though Kalena noted with disappointment that there were a lot more men than women seated on the benches. All were dressed the same in black Flyer jackets with different color patches on their collars that Kalena remembered from her lessons with Parker and Fanta. The patches denoted what Wing and Flight they belonged to.

Quickly, Kalena rummaged through her mind what she knew of the Flights and Wings. At this point in time, there are six Flights within the Suenese Military and they are spread among the three main military bases in the Suene Empire. First Flight was based at Hered, the Suenese Capital, Second and Third Flights are here in Darkon and Fourth, Fifth and Sixth Flights were located at Hotep somewhere in the south. Each Flight was made of ten Wings and each Wing was made up of a Wing Commander, two Wing Lieutenants and thirty Flyers. The Wing Commander of the First Wing in a Flight was also the Flight Commander and, even though a Kalarthri, was answerable only to the Provost Marshall.

Kalena reached out the arm not holding Kala and tugged hard on Gwidion's jacket.

"Are there any girls in my Wing?"

The lack of women in the Mess Hall worried Kalena. Also, everyone here was old. At least in the classes, the others were the same age as her. Being old meant that everyone in the Wing would be taller than her as well and Kalena and Kala hated being towered over. Videan did it to her all the time back home when he was in the bullying mood.

Gwidion stopped so suddenly in front of her that Kalena had to stop herself from running straight into him. He swung around to face her and motioned awkwardly with his plate-laden arms for Kalena to remove the bread that was stuffed into his mouth. Kalena quickly finished the remains of the slice of bread she was munching and plucked the crust from Gwidion's mouth. The Wing Lieutenant quickly swallowed the mouthful that was left.

"That's better," Gwidion said as he tried to blow away the breadcrumbs caught in his beard and moustaches. "The answer to your question Kalena is a simple no," Gwidion said as he turned away from her and continued walking through the maze of tables catching Kalena unawares. She hurried along to catch up with him before he was lost among the Flyers.

"You may have noticed that there are not many women seated amongst the Flyers," Gwidion continued without skipping a beat. "Sentience does not appear very often in women and therefore especially not in Second Born. But, women who do have the Sentient ability are always stronger than men. They can hear their partner over their link for longer distances than the male Flyers and rarely can they hear the thoughts of other Hatar. You are the first person we know of who is able to hear the thoughts of men as well as Hatars."

"I was the first person," Kalena butted in. Adhamh's warning was still strong in her mind and she was determined to push the point that she could no longer hear the conversations or thoughts of others. Normally she could ignore the conversations of others in Kurst Village but here in Darkon where there is a lot of Mindspeak, Kalena was finding it very hard to screen it out. Especially here in the Mess Hall where strong thoughts, mind speak and emotions flowed all around, bombarding Kalena as if trying to get her attention. She had to concentrate to ignore them all.

"Well, was then," Gwidion corrected himself. "Look, there's the Wing Commander over there."

Kalena's eyes followed the direction of Gwidion's gaze towards several people filled tables but could not tell which one Gwidion was looking at.

The Wing Lieutenant turned sharply to the left at the first table and then wound his way past two more tables before coming to a sudden halt before a large table filled with men. Kalena who was looking at a group of Flyers playing dice at the next table walked straight into Gwidion, crushing the buttered bread against her shirt and Gwidion's back.

"My friends," Gwidion swept his plate laden hands out wide as if he could embrace the entire table at once. Everyone turned on their benches to look at him, smiles appearing quickly to their faces. Kalena stepped away from Gwidion, wiping away butter and breadcrumbs and suddenly found herself in full view of those sitting at the front of the table.

"Ah, the babysitter returns," said a voice from the back of the table.

"Not just the babysitter, but his charge as well." Gwidion suddenly stepped away and left her in full view of all the men around the table. Kalena froze. The talk around the table stopped.

"So this is the girl that put the wind up Jerant's skirts," said a black haired man sitting closest to Gwidion. Automatically Kalena straightened and tried to school her face into her best serious look.

"I never did any such thing!" the words spilt

quickly from Kalena's lips. This man had only just met her. "Anyway, the Captain didn't wear any skirts."

Banging his hand flat on the table, the black haired man abruptly broke into laughter. It was so loud and jolly that Kalena relaxed her stance, it was also oddly familiar. His dark brown eyes now filled with tears from laughing so hard turned back to look at her.

"You'll fit in well here. Very well." The man waved them over while he made room for them to sit next to him on the bench.

Gwidion gestured for Kalena to seat herself first and quickly slipped onto the bench after her setting both plates and cutlery on the table with a clatter. Kalena now found herself bunched up tightly between Gwidion and the black haired man.

Kalena also found that she was not the right size for the table and now her plate of food was awkwardly out of reach.

Gwidion had only just settled himself when Kalena started to squirm on the bench to bring her legs underneath her to give herself a little more height so she could reach her plate on the table. As soon as she was comfortable, Kalena began to eat.

"Well Harada, this is Kalena Tsarland, the newest addition to First Wing," Gwidion made his introduction around as a mouthful of mash potato and gravy. "Kalena, this is Harada Thurad, Wing Commander of First Wing."

Kalena looked up from her plate into the dark brown eyes of the Wing Commander. This was Garrick's brother? He is so dark.

"You don't look much like Garrick," Kalena

blurted out after swallowing her mouthful of stew.

"No I don't do I. He favors our mother, I, my father."

"I don't look like any of my parents," Kalena said as she turned her attention back to her dinner plate and ate a few more spoonfuls. She then reached under her arm and pulled Kala from her sleeve. "This is Kala," Kalena said sitting the doll right in front of Harada. "She doesn't look like my parents either but she has black hair like we have," Kalena said giving Kala a quick shake to make her hair sway.

"Look at his face!" Gwidion said from behind her. "Meeting two girls in one day has put the Wing Commander in shock." The whole table burst into laughter and Kalena quickly clutched Kala to her chest. They sound very much like

Videan and his friends after they had tormented one of the village children to tears. Sound very similar to them but slightly different.

Gwidion had seen Kalena snatch the doll away. "Don't worry little one, we are not making fun of you or your doll," he said giving her hair a friendly ruffle with a calloused hand. "But our stiff-necked Commander is another matter."

Harada grunted and took a swig from his cup as he waited for the laughter of his men to die away. "Well Kalena," he said as she began to eat again. "You are over young for this, usually new Flyers are at least five years older than you are now. But you must remember that your age will not give you any privileges, you will be treated the same as any other cadet Flyer." Kalena nodded as she ate with an ear only half listening to what the Wing

Commander was saying. "You will be assigned to Wing Lieutenant Gwidion Bessal. He will now be in charge of your training and as you are the only Cadet he has to train at the moment. I expect you to learn quickly and well."

Kalena watched as Harada reached down to his belt and pulled a small sheathed knife from a belt loop.

"Every new Flyer is presented with a knife when they first enter the wing. Since you are an unannounced addition to our little family we were not able to arrange a knife to be made for you, so I will give you this one." Harada pushed the dagger into her hand. "It belonged to my brother, and he gifted it to me when I was taken to become Kalarthri. I don't think he would mind if I gave it into your safekeeping."

Kalena set her spoon aside and focused all her attention on the dagger. Slowly, she drew the knife from its scabbard and held it up to catch the natural light that now flooded into the dome from the sun hole in the center of the dome roof. The knife was plain and utilitarian and looked as if it had just come straight from the weapon smith. Kalena slid the blade back into its scabbard and was satisfied when she heard the metallic click as the crosspiece hit the metal banding at the top of the sheath.

"But what about you? Now you won't have a knife." Kalena rubbed her thumb along the leather of the scabbard. Next to Kala, this was the nicest thing that anyone had given her. "Here, I can wait for one." Slowly she tried to hand the knife back but Harada pushed the blade back to her. "No, it's yours. I have another one here. There is no need for me to have two." Kalena glanced around the table and saw the bemused expressions on everyone's faces. This obviously was a surprise to them.

"Thank you."

"You're welcome."

Kalena let a tentative smile cross her lips before quickly showing Kala and then slipping the knife safely into her own belt. Harada turned back to his drink.

"You'd best eat up and then I'll quickly introduce you around to the others here," Gwidion said after a moment's hesitation. "For tomorrow you'll be too busy to even remember your own name."

CHAPTER SIX

BACKLASH

Kalena carefully placed the full stop at the end of her sentence and breathed a heartfelt sigh of relief. She looked across the table at Wing Lieutenant Bessal who was engrossed in reading a book plucked from the library shelf when she started her exam. Kalena looked again at her thick paper sheets.

She had come a long way in the four months since she joined the wing and during that time the Wing Lieutenant had run her ragged to the point that she barely knew what week it was let alone what day. Gwidion and his Hatar partner Jolar had both her and Adhamh up before dawn for a quick breakfast and then the pair would spend the morning together learning the theory and fundamentals of paired flight which included knowing and taking care of every buckle, strap and padding of the saddle and tack that had been assigned to them. In the afternoon Gwidion took Kalena into the classroom for intensive book learning so she would start at the same standard as the other new recruits who were five years older than her. The Wing Lieutenant had told her at the start that she had five years of learning to catch up on before she could even consider learning to fly with Adhamh.

And this exam was the culmination of all that work. The Wing Lieutenant had given her the time it would take him to read five chapters of his book to finish the test and now she had to wait for him to finish reading.

Kalena started to flick through her papers, quickly reading through her crabbed writing, checking her answers while Gwidion finished reading his book.

'How is your exam going?'

Kalena sighed as she flicked through her papers yet again.

'Adhamh, I've finished it but I've got to wait

until the Wing Lieutenant says the time is up.'

'I have just finished my examination with Jolar and she had just told me that I have passed with flying colors.'

'Hope I've passed-'

"Kalena, stop talking with Adhamh, you're supposed to be taking an exam," Gwidion said as he marked his page and placed the book carefully on the table. "Jolar has been on mind listening duties to prevent any unauthorized information exchange. Though I am amazed that you two managed to hold off talking to each other for two and a half hours."

"Can I hand this in now?" Kalena asked as she shuffled her pages into a dog-eared pile.

"Of course you can. Your paper shuffling was beginning to distract me from my reading. Plus I've read this book so many times that any interruption is welcome."

Gwidion got up from the desk and sat in the chair across from Kalena. He then reached across and grabbed Kalena's exam and began to slowly read through it.

Kalena watched anxiously as the Wing lieutenant pulled a stylus from his pocket and started to mark her paper. She began to squirm in her seat as Gwidion moved first one marked sheet and then another to the back of Kalena's pile. The Wing Lieutenant seemed not to notice Kalena's agitation as he marked down the current page and she felt very tempted to try to read Gwidion's surface thoughts to see how she was going, but fear of being caught and ruining any goodwill the Lieutenant has for her stopped Kalena from doing it. She did not want to be standing before Captain

Jerant for punishment. Adhamh's constant warnings about not revealing her talent to hear mind speak murmured annoyingly at the back of her mind.

Finally, Gwidion's stylus moved over the last page and was placed back into his breast pocket. Placing the pile back neatly on the table, he looked across the table at Kalena.

"How did I do?" Kalena asked as she moved forward eagerly in her seat, Gwidion's face gave her no hint of how she had done.

"Well, your writing has certainly improved but you still need to learn not to scrawl when you're in a hurry to get things written down," Gwidion said as he lifted a page to point out an example to her. "But overall you've done very well considering where your level of education was four months ago."

"Yes, but did I do well enough to fly with Adhamh? He said that Jolar has already passed him." Kalena began to wring her hands nervously. "I'll never hear the end of it from Adhamh if I did not pass. Our one aim over the last few months has been to be able to fly with each other and I don't want to be the cause for delaying that."

Kalena took a quick glimpse at the last page of her exam paper to see what Gwidion's stylus had written but all she could see were circled words and a lot of underlining–it did not look good. The Wing Lieutenants face remained immobile giving her no hint as to what he was thinking. It was something he was very good at.

Once the page was finished, the Wing Lieutenant tucked his stylus back into his pocket and flicked back through the pages, stopping occasionally as something caught his eye. He then repeated the process. Kalena was leaning close enough to feel the breeze from the flicking pages, hoping to get a glimpse of anything that might tell her how she had done.

"I'll put you out of your misery." Gwidion let a small grin cross his lips as he placed Kalena's papers neatly in front of her. "You've passed, and you have passed very well. In fact, you've done a lot better than the usual candidates who have just undergone the Krytal."

"I have?" Kalena uttered in relief.

"Certainly you have, which means that tomorrow you will join the two newcomers that have been assigned to Second Flight Second Wing to have your first flight lesson. You will meet them tonight at dinner."

'Adhamh, guess what?'

'What?' Adhamh asked without much curiosity.

'Give me some more enthusiasm Adhamh. It can't be that obvious.'

'From the sound of your voice I have an idea of what you are going to tell me but just go ahead and tell me anyway.'

'I've passed the exam, we can fly together!'

'Did the Wing Lieutenant tell you the other news?' Adhamh asked.

'Yes, he did. Finally, we get to meet some new people. I'm to meet the two riders tonight at dinner and the Hatar tomorrow. How about you?'

'I've already met Trar and Motta. I'll meet the riders at our first lesson tomorrow.'

Kalena arrived late to the Dining Hall for dinner. She had gone to see Adhamh straight after Wing Lieutenant Bessal had released her after the exam. Kalena was also hoping to get a glimpse of the two Hatar newcomers to Second Wing but they had both gone to their lair to rest. *'After all'* Adhamh told her, *'They had only undergone the Krytal the day before.'*

Kalena was disappointed but the Hatar'le'margarten that were in the Hatar Common Room assured her that she should be patient and wait to meet them tomorrow.

When she got back to her room, Kalena reported everything that had happened to Kala who sat perched at the foot of her bed waiting for her to come home. Over the last few months, Kalena had slowly stopped carrying Kala everywhere with her. Kalena's need to have Kala near was no longer a pressing necessity for her. The members of the Wing had now become her surrogate family and friends.

Kalena quickly filled her plate and moved in amongst the crowded tables making her way to the table traditionally occupied by Second Wing. She slipped into the empty space next to Second's other Wing Lieutenant, Ben Ocbar, who sat near the end of the table. As Kalena sat, she glimpsed down the table to pick out the new faces but she could not see any.

"It's not like you to be late for dinner Kalena, what kept you?"

Kalena turned to look at Ben while chewing a mouthful of food. "Nohummm," she answered, trying not to spit her food out into Ben Ocbar's face as she spoke.

"She's been down at the Hatar barracks trying to get a look at the new arrivals. I expect," Gwidion said as he looked around from Ben to Kalena's end of the table.

"I was not there for that!" Kalena said quickly swallowing her food. "I had to go and congratulate Adhamh in passing his exam."

"Ah huh," Gwidion slowly drawled as Ben started to snigger.

"And what is that supposed to mean?"

"That was supposed to mean that it does not take two hours to give congratulations to someone, that's what."

"You're not suggesting that our Kalena went to visit Adhamh with ulterior motives are you Gwidion?" Ben asked with a smile as he mopped up the gravy on his plate with a piece of bread.

"Maybe." The Wing Lieutenant quickly took a sip from his cup to cover the smile that sprang to his lips.

"That's exactly what he is suggesting," Kalena butted in. "In any case, the two Hatar weren't there. Adhamh said that they were resting after their Krytal."

"Well, that doesn't surprise me. The two new guys are still sleeping it off. I thought they would both be awake by now but the procedure always affects everyone in different ways. They can't all be like you and Adhamh. You both were only out for a couple of hours," Gwidion said before biting into the last of his bread.

"How long are people normally out for after the Krytal?" Kalena asked. She had never thought about it before and thought that her and Adhamh's experience was the same as everyone else.

"It's different for each pair Kalena," Ben answered as he pushed his empty plate away from him. "Look at Bessal here," Ben said as he jerked a thumb in Gwidion's direction. "He and Jolar were both out cold for over sixteen hours."

"Why don't you tell her your own 'sleepy' time Ben?" Gwidion asked as he elbowed the Wing Lieutenant in the side.

"We'd like to hear it too," said one of the riders sitting across the table from them.

"Ah, it's not that impressive," Ben said, shrugging off the requests.

"Come on Ben, you and Zuta hold the record," said one of the riders across the table.

"You know mine," Kalena added.

Ben leaned back on the bench, his indecision plain on his face.

"It's not like it's a state secret, Ben," said a voice from further down the table.

Kalena leaned forward to see past Ben and Gwidion and saw Harada staring back down the table at her.

Ben suddenly groaned. "Alright. Most people know anyway. Might as well have everybody know. And to hear it from my own lips instead of the exaggerations that I have heard bandied around." Ben took a deep breath. "Zuta and I were out for just over twenty-eight hours." Ben's face suddenly broke into a grin. "But I'm hoping that the newcomers will break my record." Ben turned suddenly to Gwidion. "Bessal, what's their count at the moment?"

"It's about ten hours now. When I checked on them before dinner, they didn't look to be waking up soon. Which reminds me-" Gwidion paused in his reply as he slipped himself free from the table and the bench. "I'd better go look in on them again."

"Can I come as well?"

Gwidion turned and looked at Kalena as she scrambled out from her bench seat.

"You can come as long as you do nothing that will wake up the sleepers."

"Of course I won't. I promise," Kalena said and Gwidion gave a quick nod that she took as his ascent to come.

"You better not, I need them to stay asleep so they get a chance to break my record," Ben called after them as Gwidion started to move away from the table.

She quickly fell into step beside him as they made their way through the crowded dining hall to the Living Quarters. Kalena followed Gwidion quietly through the corridors until the Wing Lieutenant turned down the passage that led to the living area where Kalena's room was.

"Are the two going to live near me?" Kalena asked with a shiver of excitement. She was the only one living in her area, maybe now she won't be.

"Yes, they are in the two rooms at the end of your corridor." Gwidion's words echoed Kalena's thoughts and she could not help the grin that appeared on her face.

"What are their names?"

Kalena was hoping to be able to ask this of the two of them, but she could not wait any longer. Patience was not Kalena's strong suit.

"Their names are Holm Lunman and Kral Tayme, who are paired with Trar and Motta."

"Kral and Holm?" Kalena muttered. "Those are strange names."

"Both are from the south of the empire," Gwidion said as they passed down the corridor that leads past Kalena's room. "The lands to the south are not the same as your country to the north. They live in endless seas of sand and it gets so hot there that the desert becomes a furnace intense enough to turn the sand to glass. It can also be several seasons before they even see a drop of rain."

"It's definitely wetter here at Darkon than

that," Kalena said as she tucked a stray lock of black hair behind her ear. "For me it's warmer and drier here than at Kurst Village. I'm still getting used to the weather. How long have Kral and Holm been at Darkon?"

"Longer than you have," Gwidion said with a smile. "They've been here about five years already."

"Really! That means they should be used to the rain here by now."

Conversation stopped as Gwidion halted beside the last door on Kalena's side of the corridor.

"Now, you have to promise me that you will be quiet. You remember that headache you had when you awoke the first time after the Krytal?"

Kalena nodded.

"Well, these boys won't be as badly affected

as you were as they are older but they will still be sensitive to loud noises and smell."

"Yes, Wing Lieutenant. I understand."

Gwidion just stared at her and Kalena began to think that he had changed his mind about letting her see the two newcomers. But after a moment, Gwidion turned and placed his hand on the door knob. "This room now belongs to Holm Lunman. Let us see how he is faring." Gwidion then slowly opened the door.

Kalena peered around the door jamb into a room lit only by the soft light from a tripod brazier placed in the far corner. The room was furnished exactly like hers. A desk, a chest, some chairs and a bed. It was the bed that drew Kalena's interest.

The blankets and sheets were all messed up and the bed's current occupant lay on his stomach with an arm and a foot poking out from beneath the sheets. Unfortunately, in the dim light from the coal brazier, Kalena could not tell which way the boy was facing. Maybe it was someone she would recognize from her time in the Children's Dormitories.

Gwidion slipped quietly into the room and moved on soft feet towards the bed. Kalena tiptoed quietly behind him.

As Kalena came alongside the bed, she saw that the face of its occupant was facing their way. The boy had short-cropped hair that looked translucent in the dim orange light from the brazier and even though he looked no older than sixteen, had a close-cut beard that glittered as it caught the light.

Gwidion leaned over the boy and looked

carefully at his face. He then tilted his head so that his ear was near the boy's mouth and listened carefully to the constant, even breathing.

Through all this Kalena stood quietly, watching everything that Gwidion did. But faintly at the edges of her senses, she felt another mind searching. It was a feeling that Kalena had never felt from the humans that surrounded her. It was very similar to a Hatar mind, looking for someone to talk to. But this did not feel like a Hatar mind.

Maybe it was someone like her?

As the Wing Lieutenant was distracted by listening to Holm's breathing, Kalena carefully sent out a mind thread to see if Holm was the cause of the sensation she was feeling. But her thread fell on deaf ears. This person was not the source of the search she was feeling. Where was the thought coming from? Kalena's frustration made her terminate her mind thread before calling it back in properly. As soon as she cut the thread Kalena knew she had made a mistake.

Gwidion looked sharply in her direction.

Kalena held her breath, afraid that with her one lapse she had revealed herself.

'What did you just do Kalena?' Adhamh's voice suddenly jumped into her mind. *'I felt the backlash of that and I am sure that others would have as well!'*

'Not now Adhamh.'

Kalena cut Adhamh's connection and smiled in an effort to make herself look as if nothing was wrong.

But Gwidion said nothing about the incident and Kalena breathed a sigh of relief when he straightened from the bed.

"Holm is going to be sleeping for a long time yet. His body seems to be coping well with the Krytal." Gwidion's voice whispered quietly about the room.

Kalena thought it best not to say anything. She had promised not to do anything that would wake up the sleepers. When Kalena cut her thread without containing the backlash, the searching she felt had suddenly stopped.

Gwidion signaled Kalena to leave the room with a gesture of his hand. Once Gwidion had pulled the door shut quietly behind him he turned to Kalena in the corridor.

"What did you just try to do in there Kalena?" Gwidion's face had flushed red in fury and the icy look in his eyes stopped the denial that she had done nothing dead on her tongue.

"I did not do anything bad." The words spilt out of Kalena's mouth before she could stop it. But as she heard herself, a plausible excuse came to her mind. "Adhamh tried to speak to me and I thought that it might somehow wake Holm so I cut him off. I did not do it properly." Kalena looked shamefaced at her feet, that way the Wing Lieutenant would not see the lie in her face. Anyway, it was partially the truth–Adhamh did speak with her and she did cut a mind thread like an amateur.

"You should have just let Adhamh have his say." Gwidion shook his head in disbelief. "Letting a psychic backlash like that off near a newly placed crystal can cause permanent damage to its communication properties."

Kalena looked up at Gwidion in shock.

"Is Holm going to be all right?"

She never really thought that there would be any damage caused by her curiosity. Kalena will need to use more care in the future.

"We won't know until he wakes up. If he and Motta can still converse together, then there was no damage done."

"What happens if they can't talk with each other?"

"Then Holm will be transferred to Administration and Motta will go to work in the Hatar Infirmary."

"I didn't know. I've probably ruined his life!" Kalena felt the shock sink into her body but she fought back the tears that threatened to flood from her eyes. She had promised herself that she would never cry again.

Gwidion gripped Kalena firmly by the shoulders and Kalena glanced up into Gwidion's face. The fury was gone, what remained now was the face that Kalena first looked upon when she awoke from the Krytal.

"Look Kalena, don't blame yourself. Most probably there was no damage done. I should have thought to warn you but I didn't."

"He will be all right though won't he?" Kalena asked, searching Gwidion's face for reassurance. She would never forgive herself if she had ruined Holm's future with the Hatar Kalar. All thought of the strange searching mind had fled from Kalena's mind. All that filled it now was thoughts of how stupid she had been.

"I'll tell you as soon as I find out Kalena.

Now I think that it would be a good idea if you go and rest in your room. I'll come and see you as soon as they wake up." Gwidion gave Kalena's shoulders a friendly squeeze before gently turning her around and leading her back to her room.

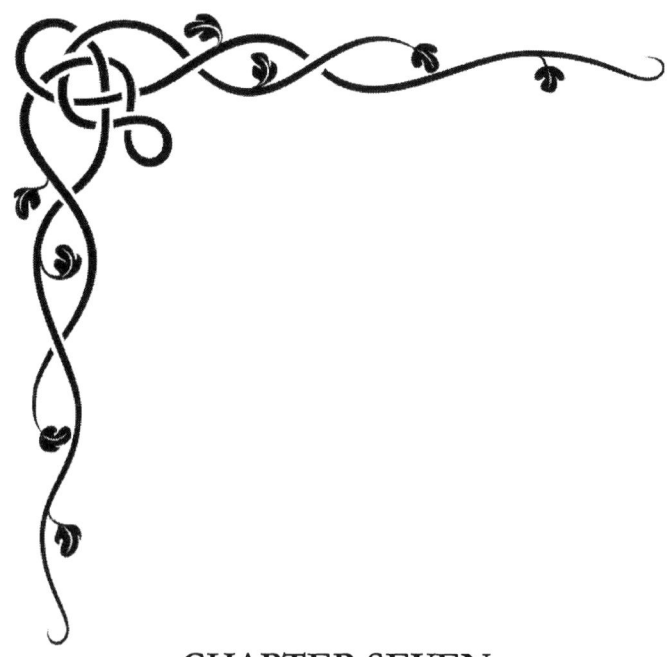

CHAPTER SEVEN

NIGHT WANDERS

Kalena spent the first part of a sleepless night tossing and turning in her bed, her ears straining to hear any commotion outside in the corridor. Adhamh had tried to speak to her several times during the evening but Kalena had shut him out. She did not want to hear his recriminations–or hear his pity.

After her umpteenth turn and toss, Kalena flung her sheets back in despair and slipped out of bed. There was no chance that she was ever going to get a wink of sleep, not with so many poisonous thoughts running through her head.

Dwelling constantly on her own stupidity was the main culprit. Her recklessness has most probably denied Holm the experience of talking with a Hatar. That thought then set Kalena thinking. If the same had happened to her after her Krytal, would she lose her inborn talent to speak to and hear the thoughts of others? Or would it just kill the crystal implanted in her head?

Kill was a harsh word to use on a piece of pretty rock but Kalena had the impression from all the people she had spoken to that the crystals were somehow alive. The one group of people that would know for sure were the Pydarki but Kalena had not met one since her own crystal was implanted.

Grumbling to herself, Kalena kicked on a pair of rough woolen leggings and pulled a jumper over her nightshirt. If she was going to stay up, she might as well be warm.

The coals in the brazier had died down leaving the room in near darkness. Kalena hobbled over to it while pulling up her socks, grabbing a small metal stoker and a small flask on the way. Uncorking the flask with her teeth, she wrinkled her nose as the harsh smell of paraffin assaulted her nostrils from the open flask mouth. She then added a dash of the flask's contents to the brazier to stir a little life back into the coals as she stoked them.

The smell of paraffin filled the room but the glowing warmth from the now brightly burning coals soothed her troubled mind. Kalena scooped a few more coals from the coal box and added them to the brazier until she was satisfied with the amount of heat before dropping into the chair at her desk.

What would she do if Holm's crystal was damaged beyond repair (surely the Pydarki should be able to do something to restore the crystal) and was sent to work in administration? The life of a Quartermasters Clerk was not the most advantageous position to be in.

If Holm's crystal turns out to be damaged what punishment would she receive? The worst punishment Kalena could think of was if she was given into Captain Jerant's keeping.

The mere thought of his name made Kalena reach up and touch the side of her face where the Captain had slapped her. Kalena fancied she could still feel the stinging imprint of his hand even though it happened months ago.

Rubbing her cheek, Kalena looked idly about her room in search of something that would occupy her mind when her eyes fell on a book sitting on her desk. It was one she had borrowed from the Kalar Library weeks ago but had not had the time to read it as she was studying for her exams. Now was a good enough time as any to start. Kalena reached across the table to the book, opened it and started to read.

Kalena had only just finished reading the second chapter when she felt the presence again. As it touched the boundaries of Kalena's thoughts she stilled, startled to even feel it again. Kalena's newly found caution suddenly flared up. The last interaction she had had with this mind got her, and maybe Holm, into a mess of trouble. Part of her self-conscience told her to ignore it and continue reading her book. But if she did nothing to find out who this mind was, Kalena knew she would regret it. Whatever action she took this time should be layered with caution. Instead of hunting for the physical source of the presence, Kalena let her mind sit silent, listening to the thought rhythms of the stranger.

As she felt and observed the presence, Kalena found that the mind was not really searching for one specific Other. It seemed to flow over and around her like water from a fountain spilling over a stone. The mind's feelers were not strong enough to topple her natural thought barriers that screened out the idle thoughts of others. It was as if it was just trying to sense who was around it. The strength of the mind thread did tell her that the physical source must be close by.

A loud thump broke Kalena's concentration and her eyes quickly refocused to take in the surroundings of the room. At her feet lay the book she had been reading that had slipped from her relaxed fingers to the floor. Silence sat heavily around the room and Kalena could feel the stillness that blanketed the sleeping Kalar barracks.

The quiet and loneliness of her room bought Kalena to a decision. Now, in the dead of night when everyone should be asleep would be the perfect time to track down the source of the mind thread. And this time she would be careful. Kalena would not be reckless again.

Kalena leaned down and picked the book up from the floor and placed it neatly on her desk. She then stood up from her chair and started to draw in deep, long breaths in an effort to settle and clear her head.

Again, she felt the wash of the searching mind flooding around the barriers of her consciousness. But instead of trying to decipher what it was whispering, Kalena stayed behind her barriers and set her efforts to trying to determine where her mind wall was being hit the strongest. This should show Kalena in what direction the physical source lay.

After long moments of concentration, Kalena suddenly opened her eyes and moved to the door. Her direction sense impelled her to move as if someone had tied a piece of thread to her nose and was tugging it for her to follow. Kalena had only tried this once before when she was much younger and was lost and scared in the wood that surrounded Kurst Village. She had begun to think of her mother and suddenly felt a tugging within her head that Kalena followed. The tugging had led her back to her mother.

Outside her door, the tugging began to pull Kalena to the left. But the left led to the end of her corridor–the only exits were doors to other rooms, all of which are unoccupied except for the last two. The tugging did not pull Kalena to her side of the corridor so the source did not come from Holm Lunman's room.

That only left one option.

The tugging feeling behind her eyes began to get more intense and Kalena felt her mind jerked to the right. Her feet moved as if they were independent from her will and Kalena suddenly found herself moving to the end of the corridor. It was as if someone was at the other end of the thread and was reeling her towards them like a fish hooked on a fishing line. This was completely different to what occurred when she used this sense to find her mother that day in the woods.

What control Kalena had over her mind search began to fray as an edge of fear cut through her thoughts. Whatever Kalena was searching for had grabbed hold of her consciousness and was pulling her desperately towards it. It left her no choice but to follow.

Her legs moved mechanically one step at a time until they jerked to a halt outside the door opposite Holm's room. Abruptly, the tugging at her mind stopped and Kalena had to stop herself from falling forward onto the closed door.

What is going on? Kalena stood stock still, listening carefully with both her ears and her mind. She stood like that for several moments, waiting intently for any sign that the mind would come back seeking her. But she did not feel it come back again. Slowly, she let her body relax and turned her attention to the door in front of her. Whatever was pulling her definitely came from within that room.

At that moment it occurred to her that following some strange force in the middle of the night, alone, might not be such a good idea. Some might even call it reckless...

Kalena reached out her hand and carefully turned the door knob. She half expected something horrible and slimy to jump out and grab her but the door remained closed and silent. Taking a firm hold on her courage, Kalena slowly opened the door.

Inside, the room was similar to Holm's room with the area dimly lit by a coal brazier. But in this room, the occupant in the bed was sitting up and was wide-awake staring at her.

The boy was tall and well built but looked a similar age to Holm. He was clean-shaven and had short black hair with eyes that seemed to catch and reflect the light from the brazier. But Kalena's eyes were slowly drawn to the large purple birthmark that was splashed across his right cheek and neck.

Luckily Kalena remembered Gwidion's words of warning before her visit to Holm–that loud sounds and bright light might cause pain to those who have just undergone the Krytal.

"Hello." The boy's voice was barely a whisper.

"How are you feeling?" Kalena dropped her voice lower to match the level of his.

He took a few moments to answer her, and Kalena could sense him mentally checking his physical self to determine what his answer will be.

"Just a headache."

'Adhamh–could you tell Jolar to tell Gwidion that Kral Tayme is awake. I'm with him right now.'

'Yes of course. Are you feeling well yourself?'

'Yes I am–just make sure my message is passed on to Gwidion or I will call him myself.'

'All right, all right. There's no need to do that, I'm doing it now.'

Kalena turned her attention back to Kral Tayme and the mysterious mind. "What were you just trying to do?"

"I wasn't doing anything. I just woke up before you came in."

Kalena frowned.

"So you didn't lead me in here?"

Kral shook his head. "Not unless you were following my dreams."

Following his dreams? That sentence struck a chord somewhere in Kalena's mind. Kalena stored it away for later thought; she had to pay attention to what was happening here and now.

"You're a little young to be a Hatar Kalar."

His soft voice drew Kalena away from her ruminations. "I'm nearly eleven and I've been matched to Adhamh for over four months now."

"Meaning that I have not even been matched for a day. How long have I been out for by the way?" The sudden change in subject threw Kalena onto the back foot.

"You've been out for less than a day. Your friend Holm is still sleeping it off in the room across the corridor."

"He always likes to sleep. Holm is probably enjoying the fact that for once in his life no one will be forcing him out of bed."

A flood of guilt surged through Kalena at

Kral's mention of Holm's love of sleep. She could not help thinking that Holm might be awake now if not for her. Best not think about it right now.

"The Hatar would know if he was really awake. They have been keeping an eye on both of you. Some of the Flyers have been betting on how long you and Holm will stay asleep." Kalena walked further into the room as she spoke and sat down uninvited on the chair closest to her. "In fact, one of them is hoping that either you or Holm will break his record."

"If anyone can break a sleeping record, that would be Holm," Kral replied as he knuckled his eyes to clear them of sleep.

"It's a pretty big record to break. He'll have to be out for over a day, though it would be more impressive if he slept for over two days."

Kral snorted in amusement but regretted it instantly as it spiked the pain in his head. Kalena watched as he pressed his fingers to his forehead as if he was trying to hold the pain in. After a moment, Kral let his hand drop back to the blanket curled slightly palm up.

"So what happens now?"

"I've sent a message to Wing Lieutenant Bessal that you are now awake. He should be here shortly to see you. You are all right aren't you?"

"I'll be fine. The instructors have been preparing us for what our symptoms could be after the Krytal. I think I've gotten off lightly considering what we were told could happen."

Kalena's ears pricked up at this nugget of information as well as a swell of anger. She was given or told nothing before her Krytal. She was just marched off one morning and that was that.

"I just had a bit of a headache but I was fine after I'd eaten something." Kalena did not want to mention her meeting with Captain Jerant soon after her awakening.

"Food is the last thing on my mind at the moment." A smile tugged at the corner of Kral's mouth. "But I could do with a drink of water."

Kalena reached across to the water pitcher and cup that sat on the bedside table and poured out a measure of water.

"Here, take this." Kalena handed the cup to Kral who took it gratefully and immediately drained it before giving the empty cup back to Kalena.

"I think I'll need another."

Kalena duly filled the cup and handed it back to Kral. At least this time Kral did not scull it down. He drank it one measured mouthful at a time.

"We are going to be doing Flight Training together," Kalena said as she placed the water pitcher back on the bedside table. "Though the Wing Lieutenant said that the training would start tomorrow, I don't think that will be going ahead now since you've only just woken up and Holm is still sleeping."

"It's nice to see you thinking for a change Kalena."

Kalena jumped guiltily from her chair and turned to face the imposing form of Gwidion Bessal standing in the open doorway.

"Wing Lieutenant. I was just keeping Kral company until you arrived." Kalena blurted out her explanation for her presence before Gwidion could say anything that might put her in a bad light in Kral's eyes. Kalena really liked Kral and Kalena hoped that they would become friends; it would be nice to have someone close to her in age in the Wing. This made her wish more than ever that Holm would wake unscathed from his sleep and that both boys would never know what a reckless fool she is.

"That is very nice of you Kalena, but you should be in bed. You still have other lessons to learn, even if Flight Training doesn't begin tomorrow."

"Yes, Wing Lieutenant." Kalena risked a sidelong glance at Kral Tayme who, even with his splitting headache was trying to keep back a smile. He covered this by taking another sip from his water cup.

"Kalena, I need to speak and prepare Mr. Tayme alone."

"Yes, Wing Lieutenant." Gwidion moved away from the door as Kalena scampered through it. She turned back in time to see the door closed firmly behind her. She smiled at the door.

'I hope I've just made a friend,' Kalena thought as she contemplated the door and the people who were behind it. As Kalena turned back to her room, she caught sight of Holm's closed door.

'Though I hope I haven't made a friendship just to lose it again.'

With that dreary thought, Kalena headed back to her bed.

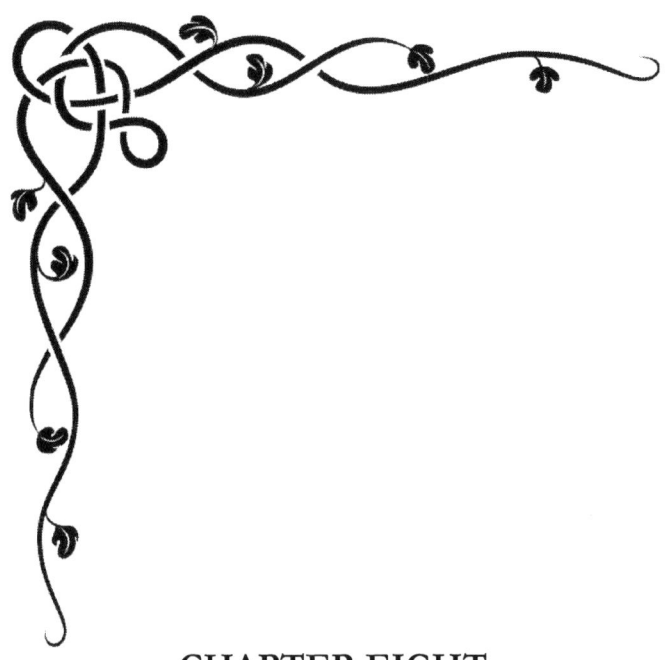

CHAPTER EIGHT

CONFESSIONS

Kalena saw no sign of Kral Tayme or Wing Lieutenant Bessal during her lessons the next day or at dinner that night. As she sat down at the dinner table, Kalena found Ben Ocbar in a happy mood. Looking down the table, she saw no sign of

Gwidion, or of Harada for that matter.

"Kalena, have you heard the news?" Ben Ocbar softly nudged her shoulder with an elbow to get her attention.

"What news Ben?" Kalena asked around the mouthful of food that was in her mouth.

"One of the two newcomers has broken my sleeping record. Holt, I think his name is."

"His name is Holm, Ben. Kral, the other one awoke early this morning and I haven't seen him or Wing Lieutenant Bessal all day. We had some Wing Lieutenant from Third Wing train us today. Adhamh was not happy about it."

"Bessal spent most of the day at the Provost Marshall's office along with the Wing Commander. Don't know what they're there for but I'm sure the rumor mill will spread it around soon enough." Ben took a drink from his mug.

"You're a Wing Lieutenant. Why weren't you asked to go with Gwidion and Harada?"

"I'm the wrong person to ask. Anyway, I think it was about incorporating our three newest Flyers into Gwidion's command. His Company is currently down by three Flyers and now, coincidentally, we have three new Flyers."

"But surely that wouldn't take all day to organize?" Kalena took another large spoonful of stew and mash and shoveled it into her mouth.

"I heard that one of the other Wings wanted to argue the fact that we were allocated three Flyers in a row when other Wings could do with some new blood." Oskar piped up with this information across the table from Ben and Kalena.

"That sounds about right, some of the lower

Wings trying to throw their weight around," Ben replied with a laugh. "No matter. What's done is done and there is nothing they can do to change it."

"I don't care what happens, I just can't wait for our Flight Training to start, and neither can Adhamh. I'm going to see him after dinner and we're going to practice our theory together." Kalena quickly finished the rest of her meal and pushed the plate to the middle of the table for the Kitchen Kalarthri to clean up later.

"Kalena, you do realize that reading the books and knowing the theory does not always make you a good Flyer," Ben said as Kalena slipped out from the bench.

"We'll see Ben. We'll see." With that passing shot, Kalena left the Dining Hall.

'Adhamh, I'm here.'

'I can see that.' Adhamh turned as Kalena twitched open the large leather curtain that screened the Hatar's room from the corridor and poked her head into Adhamh's quarters. *'At least you sound in a better mood than you have been all day.'*

Kalena shrugged in response as she let the leather curtain slip away from her as she moved into the room. *'Food always puts me in a better mood Adhamh.'*

'Does that mean you are going to tell me about what exactly happened last night?' Adhamh rose from his bed in the corner of the room and went to drink from the large water tank that sat in

the corner by the entrance.

Kalena sat on the bench by the other side of the leather curtain and watched as Adhamh's black feathers caught the light in a glitter of green and blue highlights.

'I'm surprised that Jolar hasn't told you all the gory details about what happened.'

'I felt you do something–unexpected–last night and Jolar has not mentioned much to me except that the other newcomer had not yet awoken. Whatever that unexpected thing was had you upset for the rest of the night.'

Adhamh finished his drink and shook the water from his beak like a dog shaking itself after a swim.

Kalena tucked her hands under her thighs and began to swing her legs back and forth; a nervous habit that Kalena was trying to train herself out of. But the urge to talk and confide in someone was so strong that if she kept it bottled up much longer she would go crazy in the endless circle of her doubts, recriminations and excuses. She could not confide to Gwidion about what happened yesterday. That would involve revealing a lot more truth than she was willing to give. If she could not trust Adhamh who, because of the Krytal, was now an intrinsic part of her for the rest of their lives; then whom can she trust?

A large sigh escaped Kalena's lips. If one person is to think her an idiot after she told her story, then Adhamh is the best one to tell it to.

'As you are probably well aware, I did something stupid last night.'

Kalena glanced up to see Adhamh's brilliant

blue eyes staring at her. He moved gracefully away from the water tank to sit comfortably on the floor in the center of the room. Through all this, the Hatar's eyes did not leave hers. Kalena knew through experience that this was the Hatar way of giving a speaker their undivided attention, but that gaze, when pressed on someone not used to Hatar ways, would make them feel they were going to become the next meal of a predator.

'I felt a strange presence when Gwidion and I went to visit the two new Kalar. It was when Gwidion was checking Holm when I felt it first.' Kalena then went on to describe to Adhamh everything that had happened during her visit to Holm Lunman and then her search that lead Kalena to Kral Tayme. At no point during the telling did Adhamh interrupt her with a question or to criticize

her actions. That alone encouraged Kalena to tell everything. Usually, the Hatar had the bad habit of criticizing everyone and everything, including herself.

When Kalena finished her telling, she watched as Adhamh tapped a fore claw on the ground in thought. His eyes still stared at her, but Kalena knew his mind was elsewhere. She could hear the fast echo of his thoughts as they buzzed around them but she could no more catch their meaning than she could a diving falcon.

'I think Kral Tayme gave you the answer to who the identity of the searching mind is.'

"He did?" Kalena was so surprised at Adhamh's words that she spoke aloud. It was an act of rudeness to speak aloud while in conversation with a Hatar unless you were translating to a non

Hatar Kalar.

'Yes, he did,' Adhamh replied ignoring Kalena's breach in etiquette. *'And deep down, you yourself heard his answer, though I doubt the boy himself knew what he was doing.'*

'I'm sorry Adhamh. I don't understand what you are trying to tell me.' Kalena stopped the swinging of her legs, more than a little miffed at Adhamh's remark that she should know who the searching mind belonged to.

Adhamh's triple set of eyelids blinked in surprise.

'Kral Tayme is the owner of your searching mind and that means he has the same ability that you have of being able to hear and be heard by other human minds. But he was telling a truth when he said that you must have followed his dreams. I

think this skill only awakens in him when Kral Tayme sleeps and dreams. The fact that he seems to have no knowledge of what he had done to call you testifies to the fact that the Gift lies dormant when he is awake.'

Kalena stared incredulously at Adhamh. *'You got all that from my telling?'*

'What you describe sounds very similar to the Dal'lemarden. It is a very rare condition that occurs in hatchlings. Normally the hatchling would be considered as mute–unable to communicate to other Hatar through mind voice, but when they sleep something unlocks within their mind that allows them to broadcast to all and sundry. Usually either a dream or a subject that has been weighing on their mind during the day.' Adhamh stretched out a feathered wing as he spoke to relieve a cramp

in his shoulder.

'Is there something we can do to help him?'
Kalena felt a thrill go through her as it dawned on her that there was someone else with the same ability in the world.

'Kalena, there is not much that can be done. In Hatar, this is usually corrected before they mature out of the hatchling phase. If for some reason this was not corrected before the Hatchling reaches adolescence, then the only option is to Shield its thoughts so that it will not intrude or affect the minds of others.'

'But Kral is human, not Hatar.' Kalena stated. There was a hint of desperation in her voice. *'One day he will broadcast in his sleep and find a mind that will not like what it feels and he might end up in the position that we ourselves are trying*

to avoid.'

'I'm surprised that that hasn't happened as yet, and that leads me to suspect that the Krytal has enhanced an ability that was not strong in him in the first place.' Adhamh started tapping his fore claw again and its click-click on the floor seemed to beat out the rhythm of his thoughts.

'Does that mean we can help him?' Kalena jumped from the bench and moved to sit cross-legged next to Adhamh on the floor. Absently she stretched out her hand and gently stroked Adhamh's shoulder feathers. They felt cool to the touch and flowed underneath her hand like soft silk.

'We cannot. But Kral's partner Trar can.'

Kalena's hand suddenly stopped its stroking. *'How?'*

Adhamh cocked his head and twisted it to

get a better view of her with his closest eye. *'Trar will be able to place a type of Shield round Kral's sleeping thoughts to stop them being heard by others.'*

'But you said that it could be corrected.'

'Only if the mind has not matured into adolescence. Human minds are not that dissimilar to Hatar ones. Damage can occur very easily in an adolescent mind if someone not familiar with the proper techniques starts poking around.'

Adhamh's eye narrowed as he spoke and Kalena got the distinct impression that he was warning her off of doing anything irresponsible.

'Never fear Adhamh. After what happened last night I don't think I'll ever try to experiment again.'

'Good. I'll have Trar start setting up Kral's

Thought Shield straight away and we better start revising the theory of paired flight.'

Kalena groaned but gave Adhamh a reluctant nod of agreement. Study was now the last thing on her mind and even the thought of Ben Ocbar being proved wrong about flying theory getting you nowhere did not improve on that. As Adhamh started to inform Trar about her new partner, Kalena slowly got to her feet and retrieved the books they would need for their study from Adhamh's worktable.

CHAPTER NINE

THE GRAND TOUR

The next morning Wing Lieutenant Bessal bought Kalena the news that today was a Free Day. Gwidion also gave Kalena a warning. "Even though today is a Free Day, I don't want you moping about near Holm Lunman. He just needs time to adjust himself to the Krytal Crystal and the feel of having the link to Motta…"

As the Wing Lieutenant spoke, Kalena felt a brush of his surface thoughts against her mind. *'I'm hoping that Motta will help him wake, if not then we'll have to find some of that Sardom Lily bulb that the Pydarki use to try to heal the crystal.'* Kalena quickly threw up her mental shields so that Gwidion could not detect her eavesdropping.

"…Kral Tayme, on the other hand, is in my opinion, healthy enough for you to harass him. Just don't get him into trouble."

As soon as the Wing Lieutenant was gone, Kalena grabbed her black cadet jacket and left her room with a quick goodbye to Kala. Kalena rushed to the end of the corridor and knocked hurriedly on Kral Tayme's door.

After a few moments of anxious waiting, Kalena heard the clicking of the door handle being turned and she pushed herself through it before it even had a chance to open properly.

"What the..?"

Kalena looked back in time to see Kral stumble away from the swinging door, his surprise clear on his face.

"Sorry about that," she said in embarrassment.

Kral closed the door and finished pushing his limbs through arms of the jumper that hung around his neck. "Don't worry about it."

"The Wing Lieutenant just told me that we have a Free Day today and I thought that maybe I could show you around and introduce you to some of the other members of First Wing."

"Can we have breakfast first?" Kral asked as he sat in a chair by the door and pulled boots over his socked feet.

"Of course. It was going to be our first place to go. Have you been to the Dining Hall yet?" Kalena's words tumbled out of her mouth infected by her excitement. A Free Day was not often given to the Hatar Kalar and Kalena was thrilled that she might be able to spend it with someone near her own age.

"No, this room is all I have seen of the barracks since the Krytal. Not that we got to see very much in the Children's Quarter either." Kral muttered this last statement but Kalena clearly heard it.

"I wasn't in the Children's Quarter long enough to see much of it. As soon as the Free

Officers knew what I could do, they made me a Hatar Kalar to take the Gift away."

"What could you do to make them want to do that?"

"I could read and talk to other peoples' minds whether they held the Talent for it or not. Some of the officers, Captain Jerant especially, did not like it."

"Captain Jerant is a nasty little prig of a man isn't he," Kral said as he lifted his black jacket from its wall hook.

Kalena felt her smile before she realized it was there. Someone else who did not like Captain Jerant!

"Yes he is, and that's why I try to avoid him at all costs. The Captain gives me the impression that he's always watching me. He makes me uncomfortable."

"He and his lap dogs are enough to make any sane person uncomfortable," Kral replied as he shrugged himself into his jacket.

"Aren't you going to ask me the usual question?"

"What is the 'usual question'?"

"Whether I can still read others thoughts?"

"If you could still do that, then you would know that I am starving and would like to be shown where the Dining Hall is and would not be here taking with me." A smile took the sting out of Kral's words and reassured Kalena that her and Adhamh's secret could stay safe. For some reason deep inside her, Kalena did not want to start this friendship off with a lie.

"Let's go then."

Kalena spent most of the morning showing Kral around the Hatar Kalar Quarter. First on Kalena's tour was the Dining Hall. The Hall was nearly empty as the two cadets had arrived after the main breakfast hour. The Free Day looked to have drawn everyone away to their own pursuits. The first four wings of Second Flight shared this Dining Hall; Kalena showed Kral the First Wing table and pointed out the tables that belonged to the other Wings.

Kalena then showed Kral the Training Hall that stood next to their barracks. The Hall was large enough to train Human and Hatar together with the large classrooms lining the central open training arena where Hatar Kalar pairs are taught to act together as a fighting team. She then showed Kral the Armory that was on the far side of the Training

Arena. The room was locked up tight as the Training Sergeant kept the keys but there was one iron-barred window set to the left side of the door that allowed the two to look within the room.

As soon as Kral Tayme laid eyes on the Hatar Lances and the large compound horn bows, he could not contain his excitement.

"Look at how large those lances are, and the bows; I wonder what poundage they are?"

"These are only used in training here in the hall. Wing Lieutenant Bessal told me that these are all various weights and draw strength to help strengthen and accustom cadet muscles to be able to use the standard combat lances and bows." Kalena stepped back from the window as Kral pressed himself closer to the iron bars to try to see further into the room. "There are swords, spears and quarterstaves in there as well. They are the only weapons that I've been allowed to train with so far. Did you get to use any before the Krytal?"

Kalena's fast flowing descriptions and questions did not distract Kral's attention from the Armory. What could be so interesting in looking at stacks of wood and metal?

"Holm and I were working with swords and quarterstaves but not the spear. We had also started to train in hand to hand combat as well." Kral slowly stepped back from the window. "Have you started to learn hand to hand yet?"

"I've learnt some basic hand to hand, along with the other weapon forms. But the bulk of my training since my Krytal has been in getting my academic standard up to scratch."

After leaving the Training Hall, Kalena

showed Kral where the Hatar Barracks are. Understandably these were empty as the Hatar themselves took advantage of a Free Day. Kalena knew that Adhamh and a few of his neighbors had found a nice warm stretch of sand near the Flying Field to have a nice long dirt bath. It was supposedly good for getting rid of ticks and mites that decided to make a home among the Hatars' feathers. Kalena did not understand why dirt was good for this, but she did not have to deal with the upkeep of feathers of her own–so what would she know.

Trar, Kral's Hatar partner was fluffing herself in the sand as well, so it was decided that they both go to the Flying Field to visit with their friends. On the way, Kalena pointed out to Kral the Provost Marshall's office and the Flight

Administration office. Both were shut up tight. Once they came pass the Flight Office, the thoroughfare opened up to a huge flat area of hard packed earth that was entirely bordered by the usual white washed rocks.

"This is the Flying Field," Kalena said as she marched onto the field closely followed by Kral. "This is where the wings form up for missions and assignments. Also, this is the only place where Hatar Kalar are allowed to fly from and land."

"Why is that?" Kral asked as he looked about at the emptiness around the field. The Flying Field is located on the edge of the Darkon encampment. "The Hatar can land and take off from anywhere where there is room enough for them to stand. If they are on important business, then they should land as close as possible to where that business is."

Kalena let a small smile touch her lips though Kral could not see it from his position behind her. "The Freemen do not like us, and they especially do not like the Hatar'le'margarten Kral. They prefer to keep them as far away from their area as possible. They also say that the Hatar scare the life out of their horses–which they do. Though if the Justicars did not keep a one man office here, the Provost Marshall would be a little more relaxed about that rule."

The Justicars are the enforcers of the law and values of the Empire of Suene. All of which have been carefully scribed into the Great Book that holds all the precedents for the nations many legal codes. The Justicars are a grim group of Freemen who strut around pompously in their long black robes and they have a large chip on their shoulders about the Hatar Kalarthri. The idea that a subservient class should be held in such high regard in the eyes of the Royal Family really sets their class snobbery on edge. As yet Kalena had not had a run in with Darkon's Justicar but she had heard plenty of stories about them from the other Flyers.

They had not yet walked halfway across the field when they saw a flash of color coming from the sand hills at the far edge of the Flying Field.

"There are the Hatar over there in the sand hills," Kalena said raising a hand to help shield her eyes from the bright morning sun. "They look to be having a nice relaxing time." As Kalena focused her attention on the group of Hatar'le'margarten, she began to sense their surface thoughts. Adhamh's thoughts were stronger than those of the other three Hatar and all were thinking about how nice the sun felt against the red sand. Adhamh's thoughts suited Kalena well. If he was happy and comfortable, then he might be more susceptible to what she had in mind to do this afternoon. Kalena had been carefully shielding part of her thoughts from him all morning so that he did not have time to think of any objections to what she had planned. Adhamh is a bit of a stickler for the rules and had put a damper on many of Kalena's ideas and doings that he viewed as being beyond his understanding of the Rules.

'Hopefully, he will not put a damper on this idea,' Kalena thought as she strode over the last of the Flying Field and into the sand hills.

"Kalena, what's the hurry?"

Kalena heard Kral panting behind her. For a

brief moment, she had forgotten he was there as she pondered all of the many arguments that Adhamh could throw against her plans.

"Sorry Kral. My mind was elsewhere for a moment."

Kalena stopped, letting the fine red sand of the hills slide and settle like water around her feet as she waited for Kral to catch up to her.

"You look a bit like a girl on a mission."

Kral halted next to her, kicking his feet to stop the sand from covering the toes of his polished cadet boots. Just ahead of them lay the Hatar who are comfortably baking themselves in the sun.

"I was just thinking about my feathered other half," Kalena said by way of explanation. "Adhamh is a bit of a fuddy duddy and hates to do anything that might go against what he thinks is beyond the rules."

"Why would he be worried about being 'beyond the rules'?"

"Because that is exactly what I want us to do today," Kalena said as she pulled her feet from the loose red sand. "I want the Hatar to help us get a jump on our lessons. I don't want to look like a fool in front of Wing Lieutenant Bessal."

"Are you saying you want to practice flying before we start formal lessons?"

Kalena nodded.

A smile quickly spread across Kral's face.

"Excellent. That means I'll be one up on Holm. He's always better at everything than I am. This time I'll at least be better than him for a lesson or two." Suddenly the excitement faded away from Kral's face. "But do you think Trar would go for this? I haven't known her long enough to know what she would do."

"I know Trar and she would jump at the chance to do something like this. It's Adhamh who would put a damper on the adventure."

Kalena brushed her forearm across her brow to wipe away the sweat. "Come on. Let's go and see if the Hatar will be in on it."

They continued across the sandhills now under the watchful eyes of the sun baking Hatar.

'Hello Adhamh, how's the sun?' Kalena asked him before the Hatar could say anything to her. Being as closely connected as they are, she could not be sure how much he is able to know her mind. Kalena could already feel his thoughts as Adhamh focused on her. Kalena felt a little offended at the touch of suspicion in them. She

can't be that obvious.

'The sun is warm and bright. I see you still have Kral Tayme with you.'

'Yes, he's our new friend.'

In the background, Kalena could hear Kral and Trar talking. Then out of the corner of her eye, she saw Trar fluff and ruffle her red feathers in excitement. Great. It seems that Kral could not keep his mouth shut.

'What have you got on your mind Kalena?' Adhamh's jewel-like eyes narrowed as he swung his head into a better position to glare at her.

'What makes you think I have anything on my mind,' Kalena said defensively.

Adhamh swung his feathered head towards Kral and Trar and then looked again at Kalena. *'Something has them both excited, and it is not from being out in the sun with nothing to do.'*

Kalena shot Kral and Trar a dirty look that went unnoticed by the pair.

'I was thinking that we could fly to find a Pydarki to help Holm recover from what I did to him. The Wing Lieutenant said that Holm might need the bulb of a Sardom Lily to help him recover and that the Pydarki know where to find it.'

Adhamh drew his head up in a fluff of feathers. *'And do you know where to find the Pydarki?'* Adhamh asked. It did not sound as stern as Kalena expected. It was also a question that Kalena had not thought of.

The other two Hatar who was shaking the sand from their feathers as they approached now took their cue from Adhamh's reaction to make a speedy exit back to Darkon. Kalena heard them quickly make their excuses to Trar and Adhamh and she watched them leave in trepidation.

'Well, no. Not really,' Kalena said reluctantly. *'But I'm sure that with the four of us working together, we should be able to find them.'* Kalena added the last in a hurry before Adhamh could use her lack of knowledge as an excuse not to fly and try to help Holm. *'I've also not been completely honest with Kral. I've told him that we are going to practice our flying lessons…'*

Adhamh snorted and clacked his beak. 'He will be getting a bit of a surprise then. When did the Wing Lieutenant say the Pydarki are due back in Darkon?'

'Not for another month. Gwidion says that Holm's crystal could be permanently damaged if he does not awake within the next couple of days.'

'Which will mean that Holm and Motta will be relocated to the lower Kalarthri Castes.'

Adhamh butted in. 'Do you understand now why you need to be careful about experimenting with your gift?"

'Yes Adhamh,' Kalena dutifully replied. *'And I cannot let Holm pay for my mistake–I have to do whatever I can do to restore him.'*

Adhamh stared silently down at her in what Kalena thought a severe look of disapproval. She could almost hear Adhamh's internal debate about which way he should decide. From the stern look on the Hatar's face, Kalena thought she knew he would say no and quickly turned her own thoughts into how she could go out with Kral and Trar without Adhamh knowing.

'I have heard talk among the older

Hatar'le'margarten that the Pydarki homeland lies to the North.'

Kalena blinked.

This was not what she expected, and it took Kalena a moment to respond.

'Does this mean you will help me?'

'Yes, it does because even if I refuse to have anything to do with this, you will just ignore me and find someone else foolhardy enough to help you.'

Adhamh pulled his head down to Kalena's level as he spoke and Kalena felt a flush of relief at his words. She would have hated to sneak around behind his feathered back and with their crystal link, he would have realized that she was up to something.

'Excellent.'

Kalena turned quickly to Kral, letting a large

smile cut across her face.

"Kral, Adhamh is going with us."

"When are we going to go?" was his immediate reply.

'We'll need to grab our flying tack,' Kalena overheard Trar say to Kral.

"We will have to retrieve it without being seen by our senior officers or any Freemen," Kral said glancing back towards the mass of buildings on the other side of the Flying Field.

'Trar, tell Kral not to worry, Kalena is sneaky enough to think of a way to do it.'

"Adhamh!"

"Do you have an idea about how to do it?"

Kalena suddenly found herself under the gaze of three sets of eyes, but instead of it making her uncomfortable, it set her mind humming.

Kalena looked over her shoulder at the buildings and streets of Darkon and she did not see a living soul wandering its streets. It was the first time since arriving in the Hatar Quarter that Kalena had seen it empty.

"I think it could be easier than you imagine."

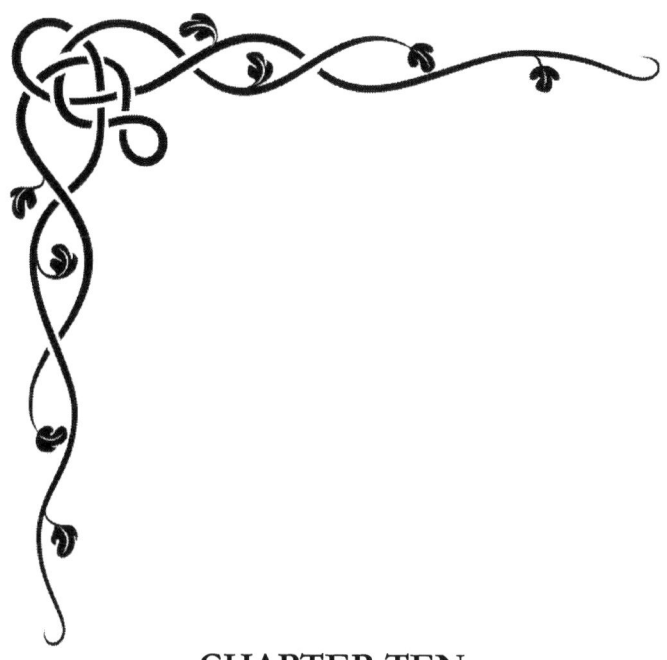

CHAPTER TEN

THE FIRST FLIGHT

Kalena adjusted the stiff leather straps slung over her shoulder. Sweat had already soaked through the material of her cadet jacket. A glance at Kral made Kalena wish she were older. Being sixteen, he had the height to better handle the long leather straps of the harness. He wore his jacket unbuttoned to combat the dry heat and a flapping corner of his jacket was rucked up by the position of the straps revealing the sweat-soaked shirt beneath.

"Let's hope that it's not this hot up in the air," Kalena said as he swapped the harness to her other shoulder while juggling the overflow so it did not drag along the ground of the Flying Field.

"Does it matter if it is?" Kral replied.

"I suppose not."

"What happens if we don't find the Pydarki before tomorrow?" Kral asked as he wiped the sweat from his face.

"I don't know. If we are not here tomorrow when Wing Lieutenant Bessal comes looking for us we could be charged with desertion. But if we appear with a Pydarki physician who can help

Holm-"

"Then all will be forgiven," Kral finished for her.

"I've also covered our butts by leaving a note in my room explaining our actions for the Wing Lieutenant to find."

"You really do plan ahead don't you!"

Kalena gave a smug little shrug. No one, especially Gwidion, was going to accuse her of having a lack of foresight again.

"Is it true that the Pydarki physicians won't be back for another month?"

"So the Wing Lieutenant says, and since the Pydarki only come and go when they please, there is no way of contacting them. So, the only way to help Holm is for us to find a physician and to bring them back to Darkon to heal Holm–Ouch!" Kalena dropped her harness as she danced back on one foot to grab her throbbing toe. "Stupid white washed rock!" she hissed.

"It's not the rock's fault that you weren't looking where you were going."

Kral had stopped at the foot of the first sand hill as the two Hatar pulled themselves out of their sand baths to join them.

'That didn't take long.'

Kalena dropped her stubbed toe and scooped up her harness from the ground.

"It's a Free Day. The place is completely deserted so there was no one around to see or stop us."

"Let's hope that finding a Pydarki will be that easy."

'The Pydarki are never easy to find. No one

has ever been to their city. All anyone knows is that they live somewhere in the Bhaglier Ranges.'

"So you are saying that it might take more than a day to find them?"

Adhamh nodded.

"I also overheard Gwidion say something about the Pydarki using the Sardom Lily bulb to repair damaged crystals. Maybe we could find one of those instead," Kalena said sheepishly, not wanting Adhamh to know that she overheard this information by eavesdropping Gwidion's thoughts.

"Do you know what these flowers look like?" Kral asked as he let the flying harness slip from his shoulder onto the ground.

Kalena gave him a scathing look which Kral, unfortunately, did not see as he now had his back to her laying out his flying harness to make it easier to slip onto Trar. Kalena dropped her own harness and began the same preparation.

"No. No, I don't," Kalena eventually said as she untangled her leather straps. In fact, Kalena had an idea of what it looks like. She had caught a brief image of the plant from the brush with Gwidion's thoughts.

'I'm glad to see you are learning not to be so obvious about eavesdropping.'

Kalena nearly jumped when she heard Adhamh's voice.

'Look who's doing the eavesdropping now!'
Annoyed, Kalena roughly jerked the last of the leather straps out of a tangle.

'Ah, but I can do it unnoticed, even by other Hatar. You on the other claw…'

'Yes, I know, I'm young and inexperienced

la la la,' Kalena said as she watched Kral fold the straps on one side of his harness and then scoop up the saddle and place it between the shoulders of the now kneeling Trar.

'I did get a glimpse of what this plant looks like. That is if the Wing Lieutenant remembered it correctly.'

Kalena folded her strapping in imitation of Kral and hefted the saddle onto her shoulder as Adhamh lowered himself to the ground. To Kalena's consternation, she found that she was still not tall enough to set the saddle on Adhamh's back. She tried several times to get the saddle on including shoving, pushing and throwing. All the while Adhamh laid still, head snaked around watching her.

'Ouch, that hurt,' Adhamh flapped an

indignant wing as on Kalena's final attempt, the saddle fell hard onto his wing joint. *'Would you like some help?'*

'A step ladder would be good!' Kalena snapped at the Hatar.

'Now, don't be rude Kalena.' Adhamh ruffled his feathers.

Kalena looked across to see Kral buckling up the harness chest straps on Trar. She can't let the new boy show her up. She looked up into Adhamh's gleaming eyes.

'Yes, I would like some help.'

Adhamh clacked his beak smugly. *'It never hurts to ask for help once in a while.'*

'You're enjoying this aren't you,' Kalena said as she scooped the saddle from the sand.

'It's all well and good to be independent but

everybody always needs help from time to time.'

"So what have you got in mind?"

Adhamh lifted his front foreleg, holding it up to act like a stepladder.

"Is that it?" Kalena asked aloud in disbelief.

'Yes. It's simple but effective.'

Kalena refolded the straps and hefted the saddle back onto her shoulder before stepping up onto Adhamh's pro-offered leg and leaning on his now outstretched wing for balance. From this new vantage, Kalena now had no problems placing the saddle on the black, feathered back and flicking the rest of the harness over Adhamh's offside.

Kalena stepped down off Adhamh's leg without uttering a word and began to buckle up the loose straps.

'No thank you?'

Kalena gave no answer to the Hatar except to make Adhamh stand up so she could slide the girth strap under him and buckle it up.

"So, what's the plan?" Kral asked when Kalena had finally finished.

"The plan is to fly north across the plains until we reach the Bhaglier Ranges and then we search for the Pydarki or the Sardom Lily."

"But we don't know what this plant looks like so how can we recognize it."

Kalena gave a warning glance in Adhamh's direction before answering. "Adhamh has told me that he has an image of what it looks like from another Hatar."

"Really?" Kral said, his voice full of excitement. "It looks as if luck is with us today."

"Only if we find either the Pydarki or the

Sardom Lily." Kalena sighed and hooked a hand into Adhamh's harness, quickly glanced at the position of the mid-morning sun.

"We better get going otherwise we won't have much of the day to search."

Kalena and Kral leapt up into their saddles, (with the assistance of a Hatar foreleg), and buckled the leather safety harness around their waists.

'Okay, Adhamh. Let's fly north. Tell Trar to try to keep our leaving as unnoticed as possible–the Hatar Quarter may look deserted but I bet that the Freeman's Quarter is not. If we are seen, it will be by Captain Jerant knowing my luck.'

'Trar says she will follow close behind me. Do not worry Kalena. They will have to be looking for us to see us.'

And with that Adhamh leapt into the sky

without giving Kalena a word of warning, jerking her in the saddle and making her cry out in surprise. With a leisurely sweep of his wings, he was flying low along the sand hills away from Darkon into the west.

'If we are seen going in this direction, they will assume that two Hatar are going to have some lunch. The very mouth watering cattle herds are mustered a short way from here.'

'Ewww,' Kalena thought, remembering that Hatar liked their meals to be alive and kicking.

Kalena had leaned forward over Adhamh's neck, violently gripping his shiny black feathers. The rhythmic up and down movement of his wings made Kalena's stomach feel as if it was being yanked out of her and she could feel the constant movement of Adhamh's large shoulder muscles under her legs.

Kalena looked back under her arm to see how Kral was doing but could not really see him among Trar's bright red feathers.

Before reaching the main cattle paddocks, Adhamh veered north and when he considered it safe, began to increase their altitude. High altitude winds are the best for traveling long distances he had said, but Kalena was more concerned about how far away the ground looked and that it would hurt a lot if they were to fall.

Hopefully, she will get used to this–she will need to if she wanted to make it as a flyer.

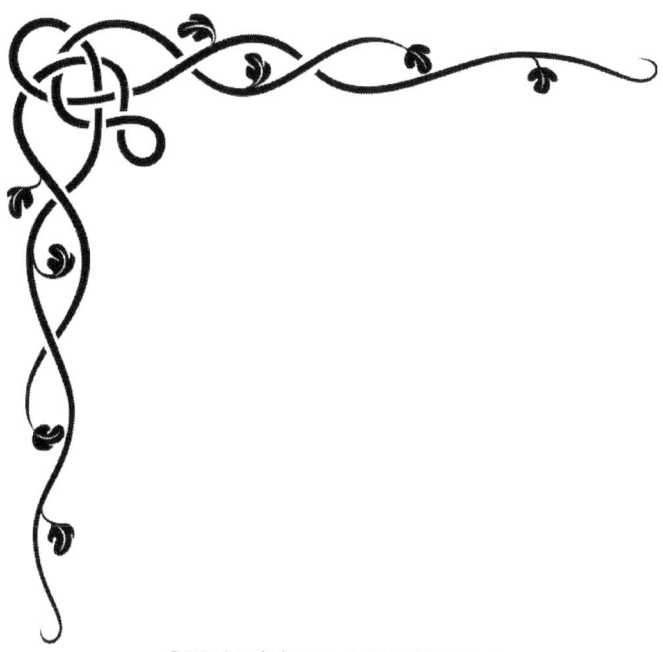

CHAPTER ELEVEN

THE SEARCHERS

Kalena adjusted her head against Adhamh's neck in an effort to stop a cramp. They had been flying steady North for half the morning and the distant mountains have been growing larger in front of them.

But the heat was becoming unbearable.

The sun beat down mercilessly on her back and to Kalena's mind; felt to be reflected back at her from Adhamh's black feathers. Kalena was sweating under her wool cadet jacket but could not unbutton it because the lashing headwind could cut her to ribbons without its protection. The land below them seemed to shimmer and melt in the heat. Nothing looked recognizable to her except the spread of the mountain range.

According to Trar, Kral was faring no better. Kalena would occasionally dig up the energy to move and look back at the pair. The Hatar themselves were untouched by the heat. How can they not feel it with their thick layer of feathers? Adhamh's wings moved in a lazy flap as he moved higher to continue his glide on a new thermal. A savage gust of wind shot around the Hatar's neck and slammed straight into Kalena's face. She quickly buried her head into Adhamh's thick neck feathers to protect it. Her face already felt rubbed raw as if by harsh sandpaper. Kalena made a mental note to herself to remember to grab a pair of flying goggles to wear next time she went flying.

As Adhamh settled on the new thermal, Kalena turned her head out from the Hatar's neck feathers and looked to the plains below. Everything still looked like a blur of hazy red, yellow and green.

'How are we ever going to see anything from up here?'

'When we get closer to the mountains, we will fly lower. You also have to remember that the Hatar'le'margarten have better eyesight than

humans.'

'You can see through that heat haze?' Kalena said in disbelief.

'Yes. How do you expect me to hunt from up here without good eyesight?'

Kalena said nothing. She was finding it too hot to argue.

'How are Kral and Trar doing?' She said for a change of subject.

'Trar is still amusing herself by counting cows down below and Kral has actually fallen asleep on her back.'

'She can see cattle down there?'

'Someone is driving a few hundred head of them to the North West. I'm surprised you can't see the dust they are raising.'

'I can't see anything through the heat

shimmer.'

'I can keep an eye out for the both of us.'

Kalena said nothing. She made herself more comfortable against Adhamh's neck and tried to forget the heat. Even Mindspeak exhausted what little energy the heat had left her. How can Kral sleep in this heat–and on the back of a flying Hatar to boot?

Kalena yawned and tried to get up and would have slipped off Adhamh's back if not for the safety straps. She had fallen asleep. Kalena rubbed her eyes and looked about them.

It did not feel as hot now though Kalena could still feel the sweat soaking her jacket. The sun had traveled a good way across the sky. She had been asleep for a while. But what suddenly caught Kalena's attention was the Bhaglier Ranges looming full and tall before them.

'How long have I been asleep for?' she asked Adhamh, yawning and settling herself more comfortably in the saddle.

'Only about two hours.'

Kalena yawned again and glanced back under her arm. Trar was gliding effortlessly behind Adhamh and Kral moved to give Kalena a wave.

'Kral wants to know what you had planned for lunch. He's been waiting for you to wake up to ask.'

Kalena looked forward again and at the mention of lunch, her stomach began to grumble. She gave no thought to food when she hatched this plan early this morning. What were they going to eat?

'Adhamh, are you hungry?'

'Both Trar and I ate yesterday. We'll be fine for another three days I think.'

'Good. I don't want to explain to a crofter why a large portion of his livestock is missing.'

'Kalena, we would never eat livestock without permission. Or that has not been paid for!'
Adhamh's self-righteousness made Kalena smile.

'What I should have said was that it would be easier to cadge a meal for just Kral and me than for you and Trar.'

'You are assuming there are crofters who are willing to share their food with a pair of Kalarthri.'

'But we are Hatar Kalar!'

'That makes no difference to most Suenese. To them, we are just Second Born–Indentured Slaves. I've been told by other Hatar that rural communities are well known for treating Kalar as they would the horse of an Imperial Military Messenger.'

Kalena bit her lip at this news. It seems there is still a lot about the empire that Gwidion did not teach her in their lessons. Hearing Adhamh's words made Kalena think of her brother Videan and the hatred she saw in his eyes when Provost Thurad had come to take her away. She had grown up substantially since then. The Wing Lieutenant had squeezed most of the naivety out of her. Or so he said. Still, Kalena was no longer the cosseted little girl that her parents had tried to protect and keep.

'Kalena, are you listening to me?'

Adhamh's voice intruded into her revelry.

'I'm listening,' Kalena said even though she clearly wasn't.

'I said your best chance to eat is to try to cadge some provisions from an Imperial Post House or transport.'

'And how would we explain why two cadet flyers are out flying the Red Plains without supervision?'

Adhamh gave Kalena a mental shrug.

'I'm sure you can come up with something Kalena, especially when your belly begins to knot up more furiously with hunger.'

Kalena scowled, forgetting for a moment that Adhamh could not see her. She turned her sweaty face further into the Hatar's neck feathers to stop the wind dragging tears from her eyes.

'If we do this, Kral will have to be the spokesman. No Imperial Freeman would believe a ten year old girl was the more experienced Hatar Kalar.'

'You better hope that Kral is good at telling little white lies.'

Kalena gave herself a small smile.

'I don't care about the little white ones, he better be good at telling big blatant lies,' Kalena retorted.

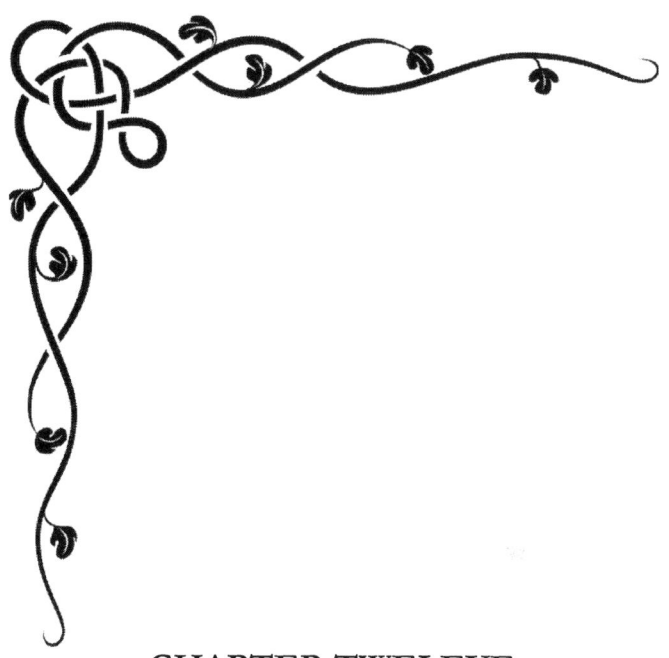

CHAPTER TWELVE

THE POST HOUSE

Kral tugged at the collar of his jacket again.

"Leave it be Kral. I know it's hot–I'm suffering from the heat as well." Kalena brushed some imaginary dust from Kral's shoulder and tried to resist the urge to tug at her own collar.

"I nervous Kalena. I'm hot, annoyed and nervous."

"Well. I'm hot, annoyed, nervous and ravenous. And if you don't pull this off, your life will not be worth living."

"You'd be too weak with hunger to do anything nasty to me." Kral smiled as he tried to push his hair into a semblance of order.

It was late afternoon and all four Kalar stood in a forest clearing at the foot of the Bhaglier Ranges. Adhamh's keen eyes had spotted an Imperial Post House that sat on the major east-west trade road–the Jaymes Way. The network of Imperial Post Houses are the communication arteries of the Suene Empire. Civilian messages are carried by Imperial Messengers who are specially trained Kalar who ride without sleep to deliver their packets, only stopping to change horses at the Post House. Military Messages, on the other hand, are only carried by enlisted Freeman who, depending on the importance of the message either traveled with a Hatar Kalar or used the remounts from the Post House. The Military did not trust their packets to be carried by Kalarthri. Adhamh reported that this Post House was a sizable one and probably supported the road to the border Fort of Foxtern. Foxtern sat sentinel on the border with the country of Arran, a country that the Suene Empire had always had uneasy relations with.

"We had better get this sham over with before we both drop with hunger." Kalena tugged straight her jacket and turned to look at both Adhamh and Trar.

'Try not to look too threatening. And try not

to scare their horses,' she said to both Hatar.

'Horse is not as tasty as cow-,' Kalena scowled at Adhamh who hurriedly added, *'We will try to stay downwind of the stables.'*

"Let's go. Lucky that the Kalar Flights don't use insignia to distinguish between cadets and wingmen," Kalena said as she started walking.

"We virtually are wingmen. They only put us through the Krytal if there are vacancies in the Flights."

"Except if it's me." Kalena tried to keep the bitterness from her voice.

"You were still used to fill a vacancy though."

Kalena did not reply to Kral and all four Kalar walked the distance to the edge of the trees in silence.

If only Provost Marshal Brock had arrived a half day earlier and stopped Captain Jerant? But then she would not have met Adhamh.

"Are you ready?" Kalena turned to Kral, any bad feelings she felt forgotten.

"As ready as I'm going to be."

Both Flyers quickly mounted and secured their safety straps.

"Remember that I'm your Wingman Kral," Kalena called across to him. "Treat me as a subordinate. Or like Captain Jerant treats his lackeys."

"You might be my subordinate after we finish basic training–I'm taller and older than you," Kral laughed. Trar fluffed her feathers and preened at Adhamh. If Kral were placed senior to Kalena, then Trar would be senior to Adhamh. They would never hear the end of it.

Kalena snorted. "Being taller just means you have further to fall when I knock you down. Don't underestimate me because I'm young and short!"

'All right! Leave the strutting contest until it is needed. You should be thinking of the here and now, not when, or if, you finish basic training.'

Kalena squirmed in the saddle tying not to show her embarrassment. From the corner of her eye, Kalena saw Kral doing the same. Trar must have repeated Adhamh's words to him.

"It was only a little bit of fun," Kalena said to herself but Adhamh heard her.

'I know, but we don't have the luxury of unlimited time so we don't want to waste it.'

Kalena nodded absently. Adhamh is right.

They are wasting time, time that Holm really doesn't have.

"Right. Let's go. Adhamh, you know the flying position for a junior Wingman and Kalena, remember to act like a junior Wingman."

"Yes, Sir!" Kalena replied, putting some enthusiasm into her voice.

Kral pumped his left fist into the air and gave the command to fly.

It was only a short flight to the Post House, but they had to make the impression that they had been in the air for a while.

They touched down in the field on the opposite side of the road from the buildings, downwind of the horses that milled uncertainly at the far end of their enclosure.

Kral gave the signal to dismount and both

Flyers quickly unbuckled their safety harness, hiked a leg over the saddle and slid down to the ground.

As they walked to the front gate, a uniformed figure stood up from a chair on the front veranda. Kalena ensured that she stayed a step behind Kral's right shoulder, the usual position for a junior Wingman and hoped that Trar and Adhamh were behaving themselves in the field.

"Good evening," Kral said as the soldier stepped out from the shadows of the veranda and gave them a quick look over. "We need to see the officer in charge."

"It's about time you lot got here," the man replied testily. "I've been waiting out here for hours."

Kalena and Kral resisted the urge to look at each other. They were not expecting this!

"Sorry for keeping you waiting," Kral said to quickly cover his surprise. "But we came as quickly as we could."

Kalena tried not to smile at the sarcasm in Kral's voice. 'But what are we walking into here?' she could not help thinking.

'What you should be thinking is, what will happen when the Hatar Kalar they were originally expecting arrive.' Adhamh's voice intruded into her thoughts.

'Thanks for your words of reassurance Adhamh.' Kalena replied with a grimace. *'We'll deal with that hurdle when we get to it. Get Trar to reassure Kral. We'll go inside, see what's going on, hopefully, eat, and then get out of here as soon as possible.'*

The soldier missed the sarcasm but took

Kral at his word. He flapped a hand, gesturing them to follow him into the building. "The lieutenant is waiting for you inside."

"Is dinner waiting inside as well?" Kral asked hopefully as he followed the soldier inside. "My wingman and I haven't eaten since breakfast."

The soldier shrugged. "Since you apologized for keeping me waiting out here, I'll let you grab a bite before seeing the lieutenant."

"Thanks."

As the man opened the door, he squinted back at Kalena. "Your wingman is a little on the short side isn't he?"

Kral looked back at Kalena, trying to repress a smile. "He is a little small, but being small is an advantage in a Hatar Kalar. The wind doesn't buffet you so much when you are flying."

The soldier nodded at Kral, though it was clear to Kalena that he did not understand what he had been told and lead them through the door.

'You didn't tell me you had suddenly changed sex!' Kalena groaned. It was times like this that she hated the fact that the Hatar could hear everything she did.

'I thought my long plaited hair would have given me away for a girl.'

'There are a lot of male flyers with long hair Kalena. And at ten years of age, you do look more like a boy.'

'I look like a boy?'

Adhamh's voice was silent for a moment before saying, *'At times you can.'*

Kalena did not reply. The smell of hot food suddenly assaulted her nostrils, and she focused her attention back to her surroundings.

The soldier had shepherded them through a small front room and into a side room that was obviously a mess hall. In the center of the room was a long wooden table with chairs and from a pot on the fireplace against the far wall was where the delicious aroma was coming from.

"Help yourselves from that pot. I'll come back in ten minutes to take you to the lieutenant."

After the door had closed behind him, Kalena and Kral rushed to the cook pot, only stopping to take a bowl and spoon from the table and gave themselves large helpings of simmering stew.

As the two sated their hunger, they spoke together.

'Kral. Let's talk through Adhamh and Trar.

I don't want any unwanted ears hearing us.'

It was also at times like this that Kalena hated Adhamh's rule of not mind talking directly. Especially when she knew that Kral could be capable of it as well. But she couldn't risk what would happen to her and Adhamh if anyone found out about her gifts.

'Okay.' Kral continued shoveling stew into his mouth. Kalena thought he was determined to finish the contents of the entire stew pot within the ten minutes allotted them. *'We have what we came here for. How are we going to leave without raising suspicion?'*

'The bigger question is what do these Freemen need Hatar Kalar for?' Kalena replied while eating her food at a slower pace. The food was still hot and Kalena did not want to burn her

mouth.

'Do we really need to know? Whatever it is, it won't help Holm.' Kral got up to refill his bowl and sat back at the table, already eating from it.

Kalena scraped the last spoonful of stew from her bowl but did not get up for a refill. Kral's mention of Holm killed her interest in food. Kalena shoved the empty bowl away from her and tapped her fingers on the worn wood of the table.

'Perhaps we could find out something about the Pydarki from these people. This Post House sits right at the foot of the ranges, they are sure to have seen or heard of something about them.'

'Maybe, but I doubt it.'

'Always the optimist aren't you Kral.'

*'I'm more of a realist. We don't want to be roped into whatever they need Hatar Kalar for. It's

a sure fire way of being caught as 'absent without leave'. We also don't have time–Holm doesn't have time.'

'You're right. We should leave before the expected Hatar Kalar arrives,' Kalena said with reluctance. She really wanted to know why the Post House needed Kalarthri. Probably to carry a Freeman with a message but why would they have had a man waiting out the front for them?

'How-'

The sudden opening of the mess room door interrupted their conversation. Their ten minutes must be up. Kral pushed his bowl guiltily away from him as the two Kalar rose to their feet. But it was not the private at the door. The two silver knots on the man's collar showed him to be a lieutenant.

Kalena had a sour feeling in her stomach but she also felt excited. Her curiosity will now be satisfied.

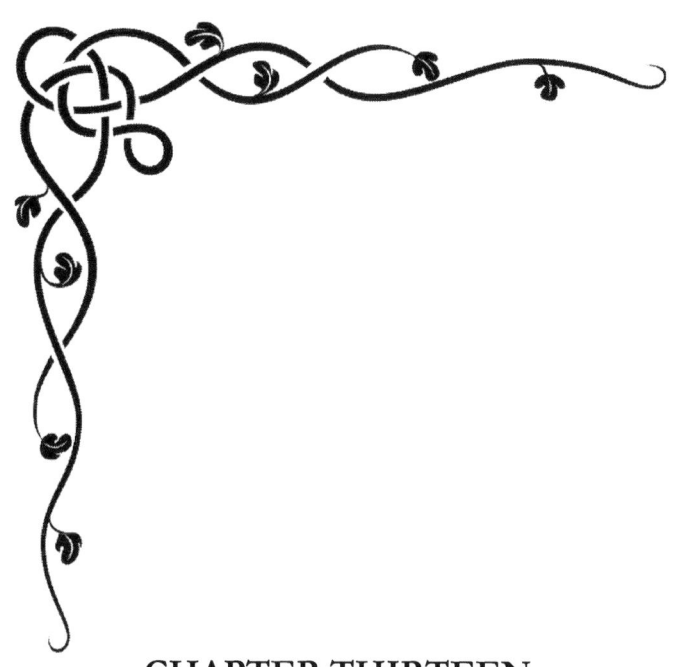

CHAPTER THIRTEEN

THE LIEUTENANT'S DILEMMA

The Lieutenant shut the door quietly behind him, leaving the two men who accompanied him outside in the front room. This Freeman was a large, heavyset man whose short blonde hair was plastered to his head in sweat. Thick golden stubble lined his jaw, either he was growing a beard or had forgotten to shave this morning. And he did not look much older than Kral Tayme.

"Do you two know why you are here?" the lieutenant asked without any introductions.

The two Kalar shook their heads.

"That's not surprising," the man muttered to himself. The lieutenant moved away from the door and stood across the table from them. "Captain Jerant's men did not want Hatar Kalar involved. But he is not in command of this Post House and I will be the one answering to command. Not them."

Kalena and Kral gave each other an uneasy look at the mention of Captain Jerant. *What are the Captain's men doing this far North?* Both Kalarthri snapped back to attention as the lieutenant focused again on them.

"Let's get to business. The captain's men have foisted a prisoner on me to hold while they finish some business at Fort Foxtern. They claim that the man we are holding is a fraud and are taking him to Hered to stand charges, but I am not so sure."

The lieutenant abruptly started to pace back and forth, clearly nervous. He seemed to forget that he was speaking to a pair of Kalarthri. The lieutenant obviously needed to get whatever this is off his chest. Kalena tried not to grimace. It looks like they wanted Hatar Kalar for prisoner transport.

'Kalena, something strange is going on here. There is someone in the Post House who has the Gift. He wants help.' Adhamh's voice snapped Kalena out of her observations.

'What Adhamh?'

'Someone here is asking for help; if you open yourself, you should hear it too.'

Kalena was not willing to do that. Not here in the middle of a house of Freemen. She would take Adhamh at his word. Suddenly the lieutenant's prisoner became a lot more interesting.

A knock at the door killed the uncomfortable silence, and the lieutenant stopped his pacing.

"Yes."

The door opened and the soldier who met them out the front entered.

"Lieutenant Ost, the prisoner has just woken."

"I'll be there shortly."

"Yes, Sir."

Once the door closed again lieutenant Ost

turned to the two Kalar who still stood to attention.

"Captain Jerant's men have placed me in a difficult situation. I know being Hatar Kalar, your allegiance is to the Emperor and to the Provost Marshall." The lieutenant paused to gather his thoughts. "They did not want Hatar Kalar involved because you would be required to report back to Provost Marshal Brock about their actions."

"What is going on here lieutenant?" Kalena could not help herself. Instantly she felt warnings from both Adhamh and Kral. She was taking a risk by speaking out of turn with an unknown Freeman but Kalena was beginning to tire of this dilly dallying around what the lieutenant actually wanted of them. Whatever was happening had rattled lieutenant Ost so much that he seemed not to realize that they were Kalarthri who had committed a social faux pas. When Ost answered, he spoke directly to Kral.

"I sent for you to either verify or dispute the claims made by Captain Jerant's men. I am not satisfied that they are telling the truth. And if they aren't..." Lieutenant Ost stopped mid-sentence as if afraid to finish speaking what was on his mind.

"What are we here to verify Sir?" Kral asked. Kalena sensed that he was getting a little tired of the lieutenant's evasive answers as well.

"You will understand when we see the prisoner. You will see the dilemma I am in."

Ost turned and opened the door and herded Kalena and Kral out of the mess hall. Outside they were joined by three other men (including the private they had met earlier) and were lead through several corridors to the rear blocks of the Post

House. This area looked to be a much older structure, made of stone instead of wood and was blessedly cooler as well.

The small group stopped before a thick, ironbound door with an impressive array of locks and latches.

"Bayes, open the Strongroom."

Lieutenant Ost flicked a finger at one of the privates who immediately pulled a large set of keys from his belt and started to unlock and unlatch all the fastenings.

"The Payroll Strongroom is the only place here to secure a prisoner. Normally prisoners go to Foxtern but Captain Jerant's men did not want him to go there. That fact alone made me suspicious."

'This Lieutenant Ost is annoying me by not coming straight to the point!' Kalena relayed to

Kral through the Hatar. *'Adhamh sensed someone with The Gift earlier and I think this prisoner is who Adhamh heard.'*

'Don't get so worked up Kalena. Try practicing a little patience.'

'I've spent ten years treated as a little kid who was told nothing and pushed around by a brother who didn't like me. Wing Lieutenant Bessal has given me a taste for straight talking.'

Kral shook his head. *'Just be patient Kalena–and don't say anything aloud that might get us jailed!'*

Kalena glared at Kral. She had only known him for a day but she already felt to have known him forever.

Bayes removed the final lock and stepped back from the door.

"I sent a request to Hered to send two Hatar Kalar to confirm whether this prisoner is the fraud they say he is."

"What fraud has this man committed that can only be confirmed by the likes of us?" Kral placed his boot hard on Kalena's foot, distracting her from saying anything untoward.

"You'll understand when you see him," the Lieutenant replied. He turned to Bayes. "Open the door."

"Yes, Sir."

Bayes pushed down on the heavy steel handle, making a loud clunk, and pulled the door open. Kalena and Kral entered the strong room. A small candle flickered from a table just inside the room. Kalena could see assorted strongboxes and chests padlocked and stacked neatly against the room's stone walls. And she saw a figure on the far end of the room swing itself up from a temporary bed made on a row of strong boxes.

'Help me!'

Kalena heard the voice echo through her mind as she stared in disbelief at the man.

"You have a Pydarki imprisoned for fraud?" Kalena could not stop the words leaving her mouth. Kral stood in shocked silence beside her.

What was once pristine white clothes were now dirty and torn, bells no longer tinkled in his braided hair and iron manacles dangled from his wrists and ankles.

"Captain Jerant's men said that he was no Pydarki, and that they had been on his trail for a while for defrauding the empire and placing the Pydarki in a bad light with civilians."

Kalena could not take her eyes from the forlorn figure. Apart from moving to sit up, he sat as still as a stone, but Kalena could still sense his presence in her head. There was something about the man, apart from his thought speech that kept her staring.

"But it's obvious he's a Pydarki." Kral visibly straightened, throwing off his shock of seeing such a revered person in chains.

"Are you absolutely certain? I've heard that the Gift of a Hatar Kalar could identify a Pydarki."

Kral heaved a sigh.

"I thought that the crystal the Pydarki put in your head would be able to… somehow authenticate that he is Pydarki."

Kalena barely listened to their exchange. Her eyes never left those of the prisoner. Then a memory came to her.

"I know this man."

Without turning her head Kalena felt the eyes of both Kral and Lieutenant Ost burn into her.

"He was one of the Pydarki who placed the crystals in mine and Adhamh's head." Kalena stepped angrily forward. "I demand this man is released immediately. The Pydarki are deemed sacred and come under the Emperors protection."

"That is all the confirmation I need," Ost hurriedly said as he signaled Bayes to see to the Pydarki's manacles. "I knew those men were lying. You will report this to the Provost Marshall?"

"Of course," Kral replied.

Kalena sat next to the man as Bayes unlocked the heavy manacles.

"Your name is Asnar isn't it?"

The Pydarki nodded.

"You were the one who calmed me when I went through the Krytal."

"I remember," he answered in the soft voice Kalena remembered. But Asnar sat as still as a statue, only moving when Bayes removed the manacles.

'Help me get away from this place.'

Kalena heard his voice, was on the verge of getting Adhamh to forward a reply but hesitated as she realized exactly what was happening. This man could mind talk! And mind talk to both her and Adhamh.

'We will just stay quiet and we'll get you out of here.' Kalena said as she made a show of examining the Pydarki.

"Kral, Asnar needs to be taken back to

Darkon where a Pydarki medical officer can look at him."

Kral gave Kalena an odd look but did not contradict her. Both knew very well that there were no Pydarki physicians at Darkon. But they had found a live Pydarki quicker than they imagined when they set out this morning and they were not about to throw this chance away.

"Are we able to take him? What paperwork did Captain Jerant's men leave you?"

"They left me nothing except a compliant, manacled prisoner."

'What would Captain Jerant want with a Pydarki?' Kral relayed to Kalena.

'Why risk the displeasure of the Emperor by illegally taking a Pydarki prisoner?' she relayed back to him.

"There are no official records to hold him, so as a Pydarki he is free to leave. The Emperor has given them the right to free passage anywhere in the empire."

'Great, let's get out of here before the expected Hatar Kalar arrives,' Kral said in relief.

'And now we have a Pydarki to take back to Darkon to help Holm.' Kalena replied.

CHAPTER FOURTEEN

HONOR DEBT

Now that the sun was down everything felt cold. Kalena huddled further into Adhamh's neck feathers that felt comfortably warm against her face. A bag of provisions and a water bag was fastened behind her to the saddle. The Lieutenant had ordered it to be made up for them to help put him in a better light with the Pydarki and the Provost Marshal.

The Pydarki himself was strapped in behind Kral and he was a man of few words. Apart from consenting to be taken to Darkon, he had said nothing. He was now fast asleep; Kalena had got the impression that Asnar had not slept properly for a long while.

'Adhamh, I'm going to try to get some sleep it's getting late and I want to have my wits about me when we get back to Darkon. Hopefully, Gwidion will be in a good mood.'

'I have some good news for you before you go to sleep. I was able to talk to a Hatar'le'margarten stationed at Hered. They had received Ost's request, and they were going to send

some Flyers out tomorrow. I've told them not to bother because we have dealt with it.'

'What! You can do that?'

'Yes, I can.'

'But how?'

'I am Hatar nobility. Being a Kalar does not negate this. No Hatar would disobey an order from Hatar Nobility.'

'You never told me this before.'

'You've never asked.'

It was a few hours after midnight when Kalena awoke with a start. At least this time she did not fall off as Adhamh began his descent. His black feathers merged into the blue-black of the night sky and occasionally they would pick up the clean light from the stars burning brightly above them.

Growing slowly below them was the orange glow of Darkon. From above, the place looked so large, it was larger than she imagined with buildings and roads radiating in all directions–she had only experienced the city from the ground and had only had limited access at that.

As Adhamh dropped quickly from the sky, Kalena was suddenly able to spot landmarks from the spread of buildings and light. She could spot the Hatar Quarter, the large barracks built for the Hatar was an easy give away and the large black square that was the Flying Field. The rest of Darkon's buildings she did not recognize.

'Pretty isn't it.'

Kalena turned back to look at Kral and Trar.

'It's different,' Kalena replied. *'I only recognize the Hatar Quarter, the rest is completely foreign to me.'*

'I can make out the Children's Quarter and the Hatchling's Quarter,' Kral relayed through Trar. *'The rest of what's left is for the Freeborn.'*

'How is your passenger?'

'He's still sleeping. In fact, he snores so loudly that even the wind can't cover it.'

'I didn't know that someone that young could snore.'

'Wait till you have to sleep in the same room as Holm–then you will know snoring.'

'That will only happen if Asnar is able to repair his crystal.'

'Let's hope he can. He hasn't said much

has he?'

'Let's see how talkative you are after spending a week in chains with Jerant's Henchmen.'

'Point taken.'

Adhamh banked sharply, distracting Kalena's attention from Kral. They were now descending directly towards the Flying Field, which now was lit up with lanterns and brazier fires for any night flying Hatar Kalar messengers.

'Did you see that?' Kral's question pushed into Kalena's thoughts. Trar was now directing Kral's thoughts directly to her instead of through Adhamh. How she wished to be able to just talk straight to him….

'No. What is it?' Kalena glanced at the ground below but could not see anything unusual.

'Someone just bolted from the head of the Flying Field towards the main barracks.'

'Great'. Kalena thought to herself. Gwidion had posted someone to watch for their return. It probably means that they are in deep trouble; hopefully, Asnar's presence will get them out of it. After all, today is a Free day where people were free to do what they pleased.

Let's hope the Wing Lieutenant sees it that way.

Both Hatar landed perfectly in the center of the Flying Field. Kalena sat up to unbuckle her straps, grimacing as her stiff aching muscles protested at the movement.

'He's coming.' Adhamh let loose a low rumble that Kalena felt through the soles of her boots as she slid down the Hatar's shoulder to the

ground.

"Are we here?"

Kalena looked up to see Asnar unbuckling himself from Trar's saddle and, ignoring Kral's helping hand, hiked a leg and slid gracefully down to the ground.

"Gwidion's on the way," Kalena said to Kral.

"Is he in a good mood?" Kral asked hopefully as he pulled his hand quickly away from the Pydarki and gave Kalena a sour look. Kalena felt a flare of annoyance mixed with embarrassment from Kral, Asnar certainly is not Kral's favorite person at the moment.

'I don't like this man.'

'You don't have to like him, Kral. Just be nice to him. I'd worship the ground Jerant walked

on if I thought it would help Holm!'

Kral grunted and turned to ease Trar's girth strap as Asnar stretched after the long flight.

"Asnar, our Wing Lieutenant is coming-"

"And your Wing Commander Kalena. Make sure of your information before you repeat it."

Kalena jumped at the unexpected voice and turned guiltily to face both Harada and Gwidion. In Harada's hand was a crumpled piece of paper.

"Who gave you the impression that this-" Harada held up the crumpled paper for her to see. Kalena recognized the letter she had written that morning to the Wing Lieutenant. "- Expedition would be sanctioned? What would possibly put it into your head that a Cadet Flyer would be able to find someone to help Holm Lunman when we have already sent a request through official channels?"

Kalena shrank back from Harada's onslaught. The Wing Commander was not yelling but Kalena could feel his anger burning hot as if it was a bonfire.

"What would make you do such a foolhardy thing?"

"We went with her, so you should yell at us as well." Kral now stood next to Kalena, head up and shoulders braced. He had not officially met his Wing Commander. Hopefully, Kalena had not ruined his career in the Flights forever.

"Yes I should," Harada glared at both of them. "You don't know how lucky you are that it was a Free Day today. I would have had no choice but to report you all absent without leave to the Provost Marshall's Office-."

"But Wing Commander-" Kalena cut of Harada's harangue; she was in trouble already so this blatant interruption would not hurt her prospects. "-We found a Py-"

"I don't care what you found Kalena. Your actions very nearly placed Provost Marshal Brock in a precarious position."

"Excuse me Wing Commander." Asnar chose this moment to step out from the darkness of Trar's wing and stand behind Kral and Kalena. The expression on Harada's face did not change. If possible, it looked to become stonier.

"Who are you?"

Kalena was not surprised at the question. In the dark and lacking his tinkling hair bells and still wearing his dirty suede, he looked no different from any other Suenese citizen.

"I am Asnar and I owe both these young Flyers an Honor Debt. To repay that debt, I will physic the young man called Holm Lunman."

Harada exchanged a surprised look with Gwidion.

"And how are you able to do that? Only a Pydarki has the skill to repair damage to a crystal," Gwidion said. It was clear to Kalena that the Wing Lieutenant did not believe Asnar.

"I am a Pydarki. You have spoken to me before after I implanted this girl's crystal." Asnar stepped between the two Flyers and stood more in the warm glow of the beacon flames in the tattered, dirty remains of his Pydarki garb. "I am Angrave's novice."

Gwidion stared at the man as the light from the fires lit Asnar's face. "I remember." The Wing

Lieutenant placed a hand on his heart. "Please accept our apology, we meant no offence."

"I have heard nothing that offends me. But from what I understand, your Cadet Holm Lunman is suffering from Crystal Shock and needs attention straight away. If he is left much longer, the damage will be irreversible."

"Gwidion, take him to Holm," Harada ordered and stood silently as the two men left the Flying Field and headed towards the Flyers Barracks. Once the two men had disappeared into the darkness of the buildings Harada turned angrily on Kalena and Kral.

"The four of you are going on punishment duties as of now-"

"But Commander-"

Harada cut the air angrily with his hand.

"Kalena do not interrupt."

Kalena bit her tongue and tried not to look at Kral. She had never seen the Wing Commander so angry. In fact, the only other people Kalena could remember burning anger from is her brother Videan and Captain Jerant.

"Leaving Darkon, much less the Hatar Kalar Quarter without permission was a reckless thing to do. Especially now."

Kalena's head jerked up, but she had to stop herself from saying anything. After all, the Wing Commander had told her not to interrupt.

"We apologize for our actions Wing Commander," Kral said in a rush. "We weren't thinking-"

"Obviously."

But the heat in Harada's voice had died out.

"A delegation from the Provost Justicary is in Darkon to determine whether to increase their presence here."

"The Provost Justicar? Here?" Kral looked appalled.

"What's wrong with having the Justicars here?" Kalena could not understand Harada and Kral's reaction. The Justicars are entrusted with keeping and upholding the Book of Law which holds every law and decree that has been issued by the Emperors since Suene was raised as a nation from the Endless Sands.

Both men looked at her incredulously. "Where have you been all your life? Under a rock?" Kral finally spluttered out.

"Not a rock but in the coastal mountains," Harada said with a smile.

A wave of relief swept over Kalena. A smile meant that he was no longer angry with them.

"Oh," was all Kral could say when he realized that Harada was not joking.

"The Justicars do not like Hatar Kalar Kalena," Harada said. "They think that Hatar'le'margarten are animals and should be treated as such; that any Kalar that shows signs of the Gift should have it burnt out of them. They mistrust any form of communication that they cannot control or overhear–The Justicars mistrust anything that they do not have a direct control over."

"But that can't be!" Kalena could not believe what she had just heard. Gwidion did not teach her any of this in his lessons on the administration of the Empire. But Kral was not surprised at what Harada had told her about the Justicars. What else did she miss out on because she grew up in Kurst Village?

"What you were taught in the classroom was how the Empire should be, but it is not how it is." Harada ran a hand through his hair making the white lock flash in the firelight. "The four of you are going to keep a low profile while the Justicar delegation is here. They are already interested in you Kalena because of the heightened Talent you had before you underwent the Krytal. I don't want them to use you as an excuse to gain control of us from the Provost Marshall. Just don't do anything that would pique their interest."

"Yes Wing Commander," the four cadets answered.

"Now, all of you off to bed. And tell no one

about this little jaunt of yours."

"Yes, Wing Commander."

CHAPTER FIFTEEN

QUIET AS MICE…

"Kral!"

Kalena hissed louder outside his door, quickly getting frustrated with his lack of an answer. She raised her hand to actually bang at the door when it suddenly opened to reveal a tired looking Kral.

"What? I'm trying to get to sleep."

Kalena pushed passed him, ignoring Kral's look of consternation.

"Captain Jerant should know soon enough that Asnar is free," she said as Kral closed the door behind her. "We need to find out as much as we can about what his plans were before he covers it up."

And Adhamh is asleep so he cannot tell on us, she thought to herself.

Kral, his hand still on the door handle just stared at her.

"Just how are we going to do that?"

Kalena tried not to smile. The tone of his voice told her that Kral would help.

"By sneaking into his office and having a

poke around to see if we can find anything among his papers."

Kral snorted.

"Jerant would not leave evidence just lying around his office for anyone to find."

"I know that!" Kalena snapped feeling a little annoyed that Kral would think her that naïve. "But he might have hidden it in there somewhere. You know, like a secret compartment or something. My brother had one in his room where he hid all his bits and pieces in, though the whole family knew about it."

"He'd more than likely have a secret spot in his quarters, wouldn't he? Though that would depend on if anyone else here was involved…" Kral's voice trailed off as he became lost in thought.

"Then you'll help me?" Kalena asked unable

to keep the excitement from her voice. But she could not help thinking that what time they had was slipping quickly between their fingers.

Kral nodded. "I've come this far with you, I might as well go the rest of the way."

Kalena grinned. "Excellent. Let's go."

"Whoa! Hold on Kalena. This time we need some kind of plan."

"We don't have time-"

"What are you going to say if we are caught sneaking around at night? The Wing Commander told us to not cause any trouble at the moment."

"We just won't get caught will we Kral. I've been sneaking around this place since I got here and I haven't been caught yet. We'll just have to be as quiet as mice."

Kral frowned at that.

"Mice aren't all that quiet Kalena, that's how people know they are there."

"Kral!" Kalena reached out and grabbed his arm and started tugging him towards the door.

"Do you even know where Jerant's office is?"

"Ahh…" her tugging faltered though she still held tight to Kral's arm.

"You're lucky that I do."

The smile suddenly reappeared on Kalena's face. "What are we waiting for then?"

"Alright, alright. I'm coming."

They crept into the corridor, closing the door silently behind them. This section of the Kalar dormitories was still deserted with only the slight shuffling of their feet to disturb the silence.

Gwidion could be heard talking as they crept passed the door to Holm's room. Both he and Asnar must still be in there trying to help restore Holm's crystal. Kalena again felt a twinge of guilt. It was her fault that Holm was in this mess, but if she had not done what she did, they would not have found Asnar and freed him from Jerant and whatever the Captain had planned for him.

"I hope Holm is going to be alright," Kral whispered once they were further down the corridor.

"He will be, Asnar will help him."

"Asnar called himself an Apprentice Kalena. He might not know how," Kral whispered.

"He wouldn't have tried this if he didn't

Kral. The Pydarki are like that. If they can't do it, they won't. Even I know that."

Kral sighed.

"You're right. I just don't like him. Something about him just makes me want to grind my teeth."

They moved on in silence after that, making their way quickly out of the Kalar dormitories and outside into the cool night air.

"Jerant's office is in the same building as the Krytal Chamber. Do you know where that is from here?" Kral asked

Kalena shook her head, hoping Kral could see her in the darkness.

"That means you will have to follow me for once because I know where his office is."

"Let's get going then. We don't know how

long it's going to take him to find out what's going on."

Giving her a quick nod, Kral lead the way across the square with Kalena following close on his heels. Both felt very glad at this moment that the Hatar Kalar wore black uniforms as it made them hard to see to any casual eye glancing about in the darkness.

There were not many people about, even the guards who were supposed to be on patrol seemed more inclined to stay inside their guard posts to enjoy the last remains of the Free Day.

They crept quickly passed several buildings where loud voices could be heard laughing and singing mixed with others telling them to be quiet and go to bed.

"I think our luck is still with us Kral.

Everyone looks to be occupied."

"Careful Kalena, you might jinx us. Make sure you touch some wood as we pass the next door."

"Come on Kral. You're not superstitious are you?" Kalena asked in surprise.

Kral ignored her question. "Just do it okay?"

"Fine." And as they passed the next window Kalena reached up and ran her fingers along the wooden frame.

"Thank you."

Then out of the darkness, the Krytal Building appeared and the two quickly rushed across the open ground and huddled in the shadows of its wall as they waited to see if anyone noticed them. But they saw no one.

They then slowly crept along the wall until they came up to a small side entrance to the Krytal Building. And found that the door was unguarded.

Kral pressed his ear to the wood and listened for a moment to see if he could hear anyone on the other side. But he could hear nothing. He turned and nodded.

Kalena quickly grabbed the handle, opened the door and the two cadets quickly slipped into the building.

Inside it was dark and quiet so the two began sneaking along the corridor, trying to gauge exactly where they were in the building so they could try to find their way to a place they knew.

And just as they found a corridor Kral recognized, they heard muffled voices.

Kral looked at Kalena and whispered. "That

sounds like it is coming from where Jerant's office is."

Kalena did not need any more urging than that. "Let's go and find out what's going on." And with that, she quickly disappeared into the darkness of the corridor.

Excitement had suddenly burst through her. Maybe Jerant was in his office complaining about what had happened? Maybe someone else was looking through Jerant's office for clues like they were going to do.

"We might be hearing Brock's men in Jerant's office," Kral said softly behind her.

"Brock's men wouldn't be arguing with each other would they?" Kalena snapped back at him and continued her way towards the voices.

As they crept closer, they could hear Jerant's

loud and worried voice as well as a soft but deep male voice with him. This voice seemed calm and steady.

"-don't know how he got back here. I can't explain it-"

The soft voice cut Jerant off.

"The Pydarki is in Darkon now though at this time we are unsure of his exact location. An informant told us that he was here."

"How do you know it is the Pydarki I had taken?" Jerant's voice rose again.

Kalena heard the other voice sigh.

"We are certain he is the same man Jerant." The warning implied in the voice chilled Kalena.

Kalena leaned back and whispered in Kral's ear. "Go and find Provost Marshal Brock and bring him here. Quickly."

Kral nodded and disappeared back into the darkness. Kalena turned her attention back to what was happening in Jerant's office.

The speaking had stopped, though from the sounds she could hear one person moving around opening drawers and shuffling papers. The noise of the paper was interspersed with low muttering. It was Jerant. Kalena could not hear the stranger. It seemed he was standing still, apparently unconcerned with whatever Jerant is searching for.

What was he looking for?

Kalena dropped her mental barriers and opened herself to the thoughts in that room. She should not be doing this but she had to know what was happening in there. She tried to hear the thoughts of the stranger first, but when Kalena reached towards him her 'threads' came against a barrier that they could not go beyond. Curious, she tried to go around it but kept getting blocked. There seemed to be something that protected his thoughts from her.

Kalena then turned her attention to Captain Jerant but was instantly repelled. The Captain's thoughts whirled like a chaotic storm, jumping around half-formed and slowly being whipped up into a frenzy.

The tap on her shoulder nearly made her jump and Kalena's heart settled back into her chest when she saw Kral and Provost Marshal Brock behind her. Further down the corridor, two more of Brock's men were waiting, swords drawn.

"Here it is," Jerant's voice was heard clearly through the door. "That Pydarki was carrying this when my men captured him." The sound of tinkling and metal hitting the floor close to the door was heard. "The designs on the metal are supposedly unique to the Pydarki who wears them." Jerant's voice still held a lot of anger and Kalena thought also a touch of fear. "They are the only things that can connect me to having any contact with him. I have already ordered the men involved to be silenced. There will be nothing that can be proved against me."

Jerant moved again, closer to the door. "I even fixed that Hatar girl so she could not mentally overhear any of my plans and tattle it to Harada or Brock." Jerant snorted. "If I could have, I would have made sure she had an 'accident,' but after she was discovered, the girl was under constant watch."

At these words, Kalena looked back at Brock. His face looked like stone but the look in his eyes told her he was angry.

"I think I've heard enough."

Raising a finger, he signaled the guard to come to him and then motioned for Kalena and Kral to stand back against the wall. All the while Jerant could be heard incriminating himself still further with whoever else was inside the office.

Once everyone was in position, Brock jabbed a finger at the door. One of the two guards immediately raised a leg and kicked the door, rocking it back on its hinges. Through the cluster of people, Kalena could see Jerant jump back against his desk, the other man was still out of sight. The two guards slipped through the opening and raised their swords, point first to the chest of Captain Jerant.

The whole thing took only moments and

now that the action had settled, Brock stepped into the room. The two Kalar quickly followed him.

"Provost Marshal! What is going on-"

Brock cut across Jerant's indignant questions with a slice of his hand. "Captain Dorrell Jerant. You are to be detained in relation to the kidnapping and torture of one Asnar of the Pydarki Mystics. A crime which is akin to attacking the Emperor himself. I and my guards have heard enough from your own mouth to convict you of these crimes."

Brock drew a deep breath and Kalena could see the strained tension in his shoulders as he tried to keep back his anger. "You will be sentenced tomorrow. Guards take him a-"

A flash of movement caught Kalena's eye, and she turned, drawing the dagger Harada had given her.

Everyone had forgotten or had not known of the silent man, but Kalena had not.

She leapt forward, putting herself between the Provost Marshall and the stranger who now had a dagger in his hand aimed at the place between Brock's shoulder blades.

Kalena pushed forward trying to make the Stranger step back. For once her short height acted in her favor. The man ignored Kalena and moved forward, raising his dagger and slammed into her.

And pushed his stomach onto the point of her dagger.

Kalena immediately let go of the knife, shocked at what had happened. The man was equally shocked. His uncomprehending eyes staring at her as he slipped slowly to the floor. His free hand grasped the hilt of Kalena's dagger as if trying to confirm to himself that this had really happened.

Kalena just stood and stared. She had not wanted to hurt him, just warn him off. A warm hand on her shoulder told her that Brock was behind her while one of his guards rushed to the bleeding Stranger.

"He's a Justicar?" Kalena heard Kral ask, but no one gave him an answer. Her focus was still centered on the man in black, though now she could see the golden book woven over his left breast.

"I think you both have done enough here. Kral, take Kalena back to her quarters and make sure she has something to eat and drink."

"Yes, Sir."

Kalena felt more hands on her shoulders as

they turned her around and she was led away unresisting, back to her room.

Early the next morning Holm Lunman awoke. And shortly afterwards Wing Lieutenant Bessal bought both Kalena and Kral the news that Asnar had pulled Holm through the worst of the Crystal Shock whole and unharmed.

Then a few weeks later the Hatar Kalar learned that Provost Marshal Brock had transferred Captain Jerant to a menial post at Fort Foxtern for an unspecified length of duration. They had also heard that the Justicar's Office had denied any knowledge of the plan with Jerant and that the Stranger's activities had been unsanctioned by their office. His name had now been expunged from their records for Treachery to the Empire.

There was much gossip in the Dining Hall as to why Jerant had been sent away. Kalena and Kral said nothing though hoped that Asnar had more compensation for his mistreatment than Jerant's banishment.

To Be Continued in Book 2

The Dream Thief

Or, if you want to continue in the Adventures of Young Kalena, you can with Book 1.1

The Cavern of Sethi

Continue the season and get cool stuff!

If you liked *The Kalarthri*, you will love *The Dream Thief*.

The Way to Freedom: Season One collection contains the complete first season of this epic fantasy saga, The Way to Freedom - all FIVE debut season books. Save 40% versus buying the individual episodes! Go to your online retailer now to start reading the rest of Season One.

Thank you so much for reading and I hope to see you again.

Thank you for reading my book. If you enjoyed it, won't

you please take a moment to leave me a review?

THE KALARTHRI
The Way to Freedom, Book One

"This Hatar Kalar has more natural Talent than any Second Born found in the Empire."

Every ten years the Imperium Provosts travel the provinces of the Great Suene Empire and take every second born child as the property of the Emperor. His Due for their continued protection.

Kalena, taken from her family and friends finds herself alone and scared in the imperial Stronghold of Darkon. And when she cries out to the darkness for help, Kalena is shocked when it answers her back.

If you found out that you were different from everyone else, what would you do?

The Way to Freedom: The Complete Season One (Books 1-5) Digital Boxed Set

An accident of birth holds the future of a nation

Meet Kalena. Taken under the Empire's Second Born rule, she is now a part of the Hatar Kalar, the Emperor's flying corps. Being paired with a large, feathered, carnivore is not all it's cracked up to be, and Kalena and her new Hatar partner find themselves embroiled in affairs way beyond their pay grade. Ice Tigers, enemy nations, internal strife and the fate of an Empire are now balanced precariously on Kalena's shoulders and she has no idea which way it will fall.

This collection contains the first five books of the epic fantasy saga, The Way to Freedom (Does not include book 1.1 - The Cavern of Sethi). Save 40% versus buying the individual books!

The Way to Freedom: The Complete Season Two (Books 6-10) Digital Boxed Set

An accident of birth holds the future of a nation

This is the complete collection of Season Two of The Way To Freedom Series.

This Box set contains books 6 to 10 of the fantasy saga, The Way to Freedom. Save 40% versus buying the individual books!

Book 6: The Searchers
Book 7: The Whisperer
Book 8: The Deceiver
Book 9: The Great Game
Book 10: The Gathering

PROVEN

The Blackwatch Chronicle, Book One

Something is rotten in the city of Brookhaven. And it is up to the Blackwatch to root it out.

All Ryn Weaver ever wanted was to be a warrior. To protect others unable to protect themselves. But on her Proving to join the prestigious Blackwatch Order she finds herself accidentally Paired with Dagan Drake, a Tribunal Mage. Theirs is a reluctant partnership. Given no choice in the matter, Ryn must now work with Dagan to complete his mission to capture a traitor to the realm.

With rogue mages and brutish blades coming at her from every turn, will Ryn be able to gain the respect of her new partner and prove herself worthy of her blade? Or will Ryn and her Order fall to the machinations of the evil set against them?

Proven is the first installment in a new epic fantasy romance series. If you like electrifying action, rich characters, and magical battles, then you'll love H.M. Clarke's series starter.

HOWLING VENGEANCE
John McCall Mysteries, Book One

John McCall just wanted to get a surprise for his men. Instead he got a disemboweled body.

A man is arrested for the murder but McCall is sure that they have the wrong person.

And when McCall starts digging around for the truth, he unearths a whole lot more than he bargained for.

Howling Vengeance. A supernatural mystery in the Old West.

Available now at your favorite Online Bookseller

THE ENCLAVE

The Verge, Book One

Katherine Kirk lived only for vengeance.

Vengeance against the man who destroyed her home, her family and her life.

Sent on a babysitting mission to Junter 3, RAN officer Katherine Kirk, finds herself quickly embroiled in the politics between the New Holland Government and the Val Myran refugees claiming asylum.

After an Alliance attack Kirk and her team hunt the enemy down and discover that they have finally found the lair of the man they have been searching for…

And the captive who has been waiting patiently for rescue.

"What would you do to the man who destroyed every important person in your life?"

Winter's Magic

Book One of The Order

Kaitlyn Winter is biting at the bit to become an active agent for the Restricted Practitioners Unit. And on her first day in the job she is thrown into a virtual s**t storm (to put it nicely).

First, she gets targeted for Assassination by The Sharda's top assassin

Second, her Werewolf best friend decides that her being '*Straight*' means she can't protect herself and places her in protective custody

Third, the love of her life still won't notice her existence and the Tempus Mage who's set to keep an eye on her is infuriatingly attractive….

You can find out more information and sign up for Hayley's monthly newsletter on her website <http://www.hmclarkeauthor.com/>

ABOUT THE AUTHOR

In a former life, H M Clarke has been a Console Operator, an ICT Project Manager, Public Servant, Paper Shuffler and an Accountant (the last being the most exciting.)

She attended Flinders University in Adelaide, South Australia, where she studied for a Bachelor of Science (Chem), and also picked up a Diploma in Project Management while working for the South Australian Department of Justice.

In her spare time, she likes to lay on the couch and watch TV, garden, draw, read, and tell ALL her family what wonderful human beings they are.

She keeps threatening to go out and get a real job (Cheesecake Test Taster sounds good) and intends to retire somewhere warm and dry – like the middle of the Simpson Desert. For the time being however, she lives in Ohio and dreams about being warm…

You can find out more information and sign up for Hayley's monthly newsletter on her website –
http://hmclarkeauthor.com
http://eepurl.com/SPy61

Or catch her on Twitter - **@hmclarkeauthor**

Printed in Great Britain
by Amazon